FOLLOW YOUR HEART

FOLLOW YOUR HEART

Rosanne Bittner

This first world hardcover edition published 2013
in Great Britain and in the USA by
SEVERN HOUSE PUBLISHERS LTD of
19 Cedar Road, Sutton, Surrey, England, SM2 5DA,
by arrangement with Harlequin Books.
First published 2005 in the USA in mass market format only.

British Library Cataloguing in Publication Data

Bittner, Rosanne, 1945- author.
    Follow your heart. -- New edition.
    1. Nebraska--Social conditions--19th century--Fiction.
    2. Love stories.
    I. Title
    813.6-dc23

ISBN-13: 978-0-7278-8306-3 (cased)

All Severn House titles are printed on acid-free paper.

Severn House Publishers support The Forest Stewardship Council [FSC],
the leading international forest certification organisation. All our titles that
are printed on Greenpeace-approved FSC-certified paper carry the FSC logo.

Printed and bound in Great Britain by
MPG Books Ltd., Bodmin, Cornwall.

The rich and poor have this in common:
The Lord is the Maker of them all.
—Proverbs 22:2

This book is for all those who believe
that Love can conquer all...

Acknowledgment

A special thank-you to the "friend of a friend,"
Karin Bernica, who is from Sweden and who helped
me learn a few Swedish words and customs.
Karin is neighbors with my friend and fellow writer
Janet Wiist from Las Vegas, Nevada.

I also want to thank Terry and Jody Fanning,
Indiana grain farmers who are related to my
very good friend Sue Dahlquist. This Michigan
author, who knows a good deal about fruit farming,
knew nothing about corn and grain farming,
so I had to find someone who could help me out.
Terry and Jody were wonderful.

Chapter One

Late April, 1873

"The Union Pacific could go bankrupt if we don't do this, Jude."

Jude Kingman eyed his father closely, very aware that the mishandling of railroad stocks and shady investments by greedy investors were the real reasons for the railroad's money troubles. The man now sitting behind the huge oak desk in the Chicago offices of Kingman Investments was no less guilty than the rest of the opportunists covertly making their fortunes off the general public, while openly crying bankruptcy.

Jude walked over to a window and stared out at the heavy traffic in the street below. Two men whose buggy wheels had accidentally locked together were arguing and shaking their fists at each other. "We both know the real reason behind these money woes," he said, turning to face his father again.

"Don't tell me you're thinking we should play the role of martyrs here," Jude's brother chided.

Jude shifted his gaze to his younger sibling. He and Mark were Yale educated, both in charge of various factions of the Kingman empire; but Mark looked so much more like their father—in his short, stocky build, chin line and smile, in his light brown hair and pale gray eyes that turned a deeper, cold blue-gray color when it came to business dealings, like right now. Anyone who didn't know them would not believe he and Mark were brothers. They were so different in looks and personality.

Smile to their faces, shake their hands, stab them in the back whenever necessary. That was Mark's motto. In that respect he and their father were most alike. Jude's disagreement with such an attitude often spawned arguments among them over business dealings.

"I'm not suggesting any such thing," Jude answered Mark. "I'm just asking why we should force innocent people to pay for the grievous errors and greediness of the men who invested in the railroad and then pocketed money that rightfully belonged to the government *and* the railroad."

"You yourself are benefiting from some of that greed, big brother," Mark reminded him smugly. "You and I might not have made the decisions, but we're living very nicely off some of that money, and I intend to help Dad protect his interests in this. I'm sure you want the same."

Jude frowned. Mark always had a way of making it look as if he was the only son who was interested in their father's welfare. He turned his attention to his father. "Some of those people worked their land for years before the railroads even reached them. Now we're going to turn around and tell them they have to get out?"

"Or pay a big price," Mark answered first. "It's not our fault they fell for the underhanded dealings of disreputable land agents."

Compelled to direct his attention to his brother again, Jude forced self-control. "Well, that's just like you, Mark, isn't it? Far be it from you to consider a person's feelings if it might cost you an expensive cigar or caviar for breakfast."

"That's enough," their father ordered. He scowled at Jude. "The point is, son, that we can find people back in New York and Boston and even overseas who would be happy to buy up that land at premium prices, especially now that it's been worked and there are towns sprouting up all along the railroad. Don't forget that those first settlers went out there with dreams of getting rich off the railroad, so they are no less guilty of greed than we are."

"They were promised they could buy that land at rock-bottom prices," Jude protested.

"No money ever changed hands, so they aren't out anything. We have every right to take back the land and sell it. And think of what we can use that money for—branching lines north and south of the main route, as well as getting the railroad back in the black. This whole land situation has been a mess, and everybody knows it. This will likely end up in court. Why not get rid of some of those people right now, before it gets that far? They don't have a chance anyway, let alone the money to fight us. Our family business has a lot to lose if the U.P. goes under."

Jude raised his eyebrows and smirked. "I suspect we've already gained much more than we will ever lose," he answered. He moved to sit down in a large leather chair next to Mark.

Jefferson sighed. "Those people were too ignorant and poor to put up decent money and get properly signed and registered deeds in the first place. Those farmers are now nothing more than squatters, Jude, and you have to face that fact. Why does this bother you so much?"

Jude sighed. "Because we aren't dealing with other ruthless businessmen," he answered, "men who would walk all over us to get what they wanted. These are simple farmers, most of them immigrants, who thought they were doing the right thing—people who came to America with dreams of a better life and who worked hard to make that happen."

"Whoa! Whoa, big brother!" Mark said with a chuckle. "Get off your soapbox. When did you become such a supporter of the poor and downtrodden?"

Jude ignored him. "I just don't want the Kingman name associated with hard-heartedness and walking all over poor people," he told his father.

"Maybe he'd like to go live in a soddy and help plow the cornfields," Mark suggested snidely.

"There must be some alternative to this," Jude said.

"There isn't," Jefferson answered.

Jude noticed a familiar, cold look move into the

man's eyes, the look that meant he'd made a decision and there was no arguing with it.

"But since you're better at dealing with the common people than Mark is," Jefferson continued, "I'm sending you down to Omaha with the job of doing what you can to get rid of some of those settlers, Jude—and just as you mentioned, without making us look bad."

Jude just shook his head. "Why do I get the feeling this is some kind of test?"

"It is. Dad knows I can run Kingman Enterprises better than you can," Mark told him. "Here's your chance to show him you can come through for him."

"That's enough, Mark," Jefferson told him, keeping his eyes on Jude. "I'm getting older, Jude, and it's time you and Mark both take on even more holdings of my businesses. And although Mark is younger, he seems to understand the necessity of keeping personal feelings out of business dealings, something you've always had trouble doing. However, you're handsome and charming and intelligent. This is the perfect venue for you to show me what you can do. I want to go out of this world confident that you and Mark can *both* take care of Kingman Investments and Corporate Enterprises."

Jefferson stood up, obviously becoming agitated, his face reddening slightly, his chest puffed out, pride making him raise his chin and speak a little louder. Jude thought how, when his father took on this mood, he seemed much taller than his five-foot-eight-inch frame.

"I came up from the bottom," Jefferson continued. "You both know that. I started with nothing, and I scraped and saved and earned and fought my way to the top, investing, reinvesting, taking advantage of good deals, buying at premium lows, and, yes, sometimes walking right over people to get what I wanted."

His words came as he paced, but then he stopped and came around to sit on his desk, facing both sons. His look turned harder. "You've heard the story before. My father was once wealthy, but he lost it all through a partner who stabbed him in the back financially!" His fists tightened. "My mother—your grandmother—died from lack of proper medical care when she became gravely ill and there was no money for a hospital and doctors. My father shot himself because he felt like a failure and felt responsible for my mother's death. I vowed then and there that I would make up for all of it, and I *have*. That included putting out of business the very man who destroyed my father. Now I'm depending on my own sons to make *their* father proud, and to never let what I've spent my life building be destroyed."

He sat down behind his desk again. "Remember that what you have will go to your own children some day. Do this for *them*. Handle this right, and *all* my railroad interests will go to you. Mark will handle everything else. I'm talking millions of dollars and a lot of responsibility, Jude. Do this not just for me, but for yourself."

Jude studied his father's eyes, trying to find love there. He saw a spark of it, but always it was mixed with a strange doubt. It was that doubt that had always made him long for approval and affection from both his parents. Here was a chance to find favor in his father's eyes, and he longed to accomplish that.

"When do I leave?" he asked, already dreading the job.

"Within a week or two, after Corinne's spring social. Your mother would never forgive me if either of you missed the event of the year." Jefferson smiled, his mood lighter again.

"Ah, yes, the spring social," Mark mused. "Mother's time to shine." He looked at Jude. "And your chance to make all the young girls swoon," he added snidely. "When do you think you'll marry one of them, big brother? Or do you plan to just keep breaking their hearts?"

"I prefer not to marry someone just for status and to add to my wealth," Jude interrupted, rising.

Mark's gaze darkened. "That's not why I'm marrying Cindy."

Jude glared at him. "I know you too well, *little* brother. You don't fool me one bit. You're about as capable of loving someone as a lion is capable of loving a lamb." He walked out, not caring to get into a full-blown argument or to listen to his father defend Mark. He truly wished he could get along with his brother, but Mark's jealousy and spoiled, immature determination to be the favorite made that impossible.

He decided his assignment to go to Omaha wasn't so bad after all. At least he could get away from Mark's incessant whining and insults, and from his mother's petty lifestyle. Maybe he wouldn't even stay for the all-important spring social. His mother's deliberate and gaudy display of wealth and importance was not something he enjoyed. Nor did he look forward to the fawning of the available young women who attended, obviously hoping to marry into the Kingman wealth. He wanted something more in a woman than her being among the proper "class" for a Kingman. He wanted honesty and integrity. He wanted strength tempered with compassion. Most of all he wanted a woman who would love him for himself, not his station in life, or his money.

Such a woman would not be an easy find, which was why at twenty-nine years of age he was still single. He vowed never to end up married to a woman anything like his mother. Thanks to her, he wasn't even sure how real love was supposed to feel.

Chapter Two

The hem of Ingrid's dress hung heavy with mud, and she dreaded the mess her worn, black, high-top shoes would be by the time she finished gathering eggs and feeding the pigs. According to her diary entry of one year ago, Nebraska experienced a freak snowstorm this time last year. This spring was just the opposite. Although she did not doubt more cold weather was ahead, today was unusually warm and humid. Only partially thawed, the ground beneath her feet was a quagmire. In some places she literally had to yank her feet out of the mud.

Basket in hand, she made her way to the chicken

coop, glancing first at a larger shed to see her ten-year-old brother throwing pebbles into a mud puddle. "Johnny Svensson, you are supposed to be milking the cow!" she shouted.

Looking startled, the towheaded boy turned and ran back into the shed.

"When will that boy learn to stay with one job until it is finished?" Ingrid muttered.

She stooped to enter a small sod chicken coop, wanting to hurry with her own chores so she could get breakfast started. Her father, always the first one up and out, was checking the fields to see if he might be able to plow some furrows to prepare for planting.

A farmer's work was never done. Even in winter Albert Svensson was out in the barn every day sharpening tools, sorting baskets and taking care of other endless winter chores in preparation for spring planting and a long, hot summer of farming. In spite of a painful back problem that had plagued him the past two years, her tall, strong father never shunned work and considered it the only way to heaven.

"Perhaps it is," she said to the chickens. Hard work kept a person busy, with no time to think about, let alone act on, sinful ways. She remembered her mother telling her that when she was just a little girl.

Hens pecked at her hands as she shooed them away from their nests so she could collect their eggs. She laid the still-warm eggs in her basket, glad to find plenty to cook a big breakfast.

She ducked out of the hen shed, enjoying the warm morning sun. It was times like this when she missed her mother the most. Yolanda Svensson would have gloried in a morning like this. Although she'd died ten years ago when Johnny was born, Ingrid still had vivid memories of the strong, brave woman.

She headed back to the family's soddy, where coffee was still warming on her proudest possession, a Concord cooking range ordered from Pennsylvania through Grooten's Dry Goods in nearby Plum Creek. In winter it warmed the house much better than their stone fireplace ever had. How her mother would have enjoyed that stove!

Before she reached the house, the long wail of another Union Pacific locomotive cried out through the morning air. That would be the 7:00 a.m. She'd never ridden a train—couldn't afford it—but she could time her day by their regularity.

She went into the house and set her basket of eggs on a small table near the entrance, being careful not to get mud on the wood plank floor. After her father had laid that floor last year she'd felt as though she were living in luxury. The soddy's mud-plastered walls were now whitewashed, and two real glass windows let in sunlight. The sod roof had been replaced two years ago with real wood beams, wood planks and shingles, so she no longer had to hang blankets under the ceiling to catch dirt and bugs, which pleased her greatly.

She turned around and made her way to the cowshed, stepping inside to see that her brother had collected enough milk to garner a good amount of cream for making butter.

"Good job, Johnny," she praised him, taking the bucket. Together they headed back to the house, the disappearing locomotive still wailing in the distance and leaving a trail of smoke on the horizon.

"Ingrid?" Johnny asked.

"What is it?"

"What if I don't want to be a farmer when I grow up?"

Ingrid stopped walking and faced him. "Of *course* you will be a farmer, Johnny. That is why *Far* is building up this land," she reminded him, affectionately using the Swedish term for father. "This farm will be yours someday."

Johnny looked across the flat expanse of farmland at the lingering smoke in the air. "Maybe I'll want to be a locomotive engineer, or ride the caboose. Maybe I'll just get on a train and go as far as it will take me."

Ingrid could just imagine the picture of adventure trains conjured up for a boy of ten, the whistle beckoning a child's spirit to explore a faraway land. "When you are older you will see what is truly important, Johnny. Honoring your father is important. Working the land is important. Perhaps you might leave for a while, but this is your home, and you will always come back."

Johnny frowned. "How do you know?"

These were times when Ingrid missed her beloved mother the most, sure the woman would always have the right answers. "I just know it, Johnny, in my heart. The only thing that matters in life is our loved ones, the land and our faith in God."

Johnny just shrugged. "After church Sunday can I go watch the trains?"

"You will have to ask Far. It depends on how much we need in the way of supplies and if we need your help loading them. I don't want Far lifting too much because of his back."

"Well..." Johnny regarded his sister. "Why don't you marry Carl? He could help us a lot, and Far wouldn't have so much work to do."

Ingrid shook her head at her brother's reference

to their closest neighbor, another Swede named Carl Unger, who had hinted more than once to her father that he was interested in marrying her. "Marriage is not something to take lightly, Johnny. And I do not love Carl in the right way to marry him."

"But he's a real good man, and I really like him."

"I know, Johnny, I know." At nineteen, Ingrid knew she should most certainly be thinking about marriage, but there was so much to do on the farm, plus all the cooking and cleaning and helping raise Johnny, that she'd seldom had time to ponder marriage or to get involved in the process of being courted. Besides, no one had come along who'd made her heart beat a little faster with true feelings of love. Her father seemed to think she was getting old enough that she should no longer be too picky, and he felt Carl was by far the best man for her.

Ingrid was not sure of that at all. When she was little her mother had once told her to marry for love and love alone. *Love, and your faith in God, can help you through just about anything life hands you,* she'd told her. Since then Ingrid had held on to the dream that someday the right man would come along, and she would know it in her heart when he did.

Chapter Three

Early May

Wilson Beyer adjusted his tiny square spectacles, studying the list of names in front of him. As was his habit, he twitched his tiny mustache and cleared his throat every few seconds, which irritated Jude to no end, even though he liked the man.

"I prepared a list for you, just as you asked in your telegram," Wilson told Jude. "And I have men ready to go out with you to order these settlers off their property."

Jude took a thin cigar from his vest pocket, then

put it to his lips and leaned down to light it from a tapered candle burning on Wilson's desk. Wilson actually thought burning a candle would some-how relieve him of some of his spring allergies. "I don't need the extra men," he told Wilson. He puffed on the cigar to get it burning.

Wilson's eyebrows shot up in surprise. "Oh? I should advise you that these settlers won't leave peacefully. It could even involve firearms."

Jude shrugged. "I'd rather try a less forceful approach. I intend to go visit each settler on my own first."

"Your father won't be very pleased."

"You don't need to tell me that. I've never been able to please him anyway. Besides, all he told me was to come down here and prepare the settlers for the inevitable, so I will handle this the way I see fit."

Wilson cleared his throat again. "Must you smoke that cigar? I have enough trouble with the pollen and dust and humidity in this cow town without breathing that wretched cigar smoke."

Jude took the offending article from his lips and eyed it a moment. "Actually, it calms me, but if it stirs up your endless list of allergies, I'll put it out for the moment."

Wilson smiled, showing dark, tiny teeth. "Well, that's kind of you, Jude. I didn't mean to be rude, but I swear, if you didn't pay me so well I'd hop the next train back to Chicago."

"Yes, the air is so *clean* in Chicago," Jude answered wryly as he stamped out the barely smoked tobacco. He looked around the plain, unpretentious office and sat down in a wooden chair across from Wilson's desk. "Omaha is growing fast," he added. "Someday it will rival Chicago."

Wilson grunted a laugh. "I'll be long dead from allergies by then."

Both men laughed as Wilson handed over the list of settlers' names and locations. "You have your work cut out for you, Jude. The people on that list will either have to get off their land or buy it at the going rate, which is more than most of them can afford."

"I know." Jude scanned the list, still irritated at the job his father had given him. "What do you think of all this, Wilson?"

Wilson thought a moment. "I like my job in land management, so I suppose I have to back the powers that be so we stay in business." He pulled his glasses down to the end of his nose and looked up bare-eyed at Jude. "Is this *really* necessary?"

Jude ran a hand through his hair, wishing he could better control its thick waves. "According to my father it is, and I'm a Kingman, after all. I have a job to do."

"I'm surprised Jefferson didn't give this job to your brother. From what I know of you two, Mark seems the better man for the job, and I don't mean that as an insult to you—"

Jude put up his hand to cut him off. "I know."

"Sometimes I wonder about that brother of yours. He has a wicked streak, and your parents spoil him rotten. From what I've observed, you and Mark are like night and day—"

Jude waved him off again. "The fact remains the job was given to me."

"Well, personally, I'm glad it was. I shudder to think of how he'd handle this. I have every confidence that you will take a more human approach. There are some good people on that list, Jude, hardworking, honest Christian people who came out here with big hopes and dreams."

Wilson cleared his throat yet again. "I should warn you that, in spite of their normally peaceful ways, you'll run into trouble with some of them. I suggest you take along at least one armed man. He can stay in the coach if you don't want to appear too intimidating. I just don't want to answer to Jefferson Kingman if you go out there alone and get yourself shot."

Jude frowned. "You think it could get to that point?"

Wilson shrugged. "It could. I'd watch out for the one called Carl Unger. He and his father have worked their farm alone for years—ten, twelve, something like that. And my sources in Plum Creek tell me the man has his heart set on marrying soon, so he'll want that farm for his future family. You might also have a problem with Albert Svensson. He has a son he intends to hand the farm to, and his daughter, Ingrid, is the one Carl Unger wants to marry. Their farms adjoin, so together they'll be something to deal with. The Svenssons have farmed their section for nine years now. Ingrid's mother is buried there. Of course, there are some who aren't doing that well and might give things up without much of a fight."

Jude sighed as he rose. "Well, as Mark and my father would say, business is business." He took his top hat from where he'd set it on Wilson's desk and put it on. "I suppose I'd better hop a train to the wonderful whistle-stop of Plum Creek and get moving on this."

"There aren't any fancy hotels there, Jude."

"I figured as much. I'll be staying in my private Pullman. It has everything I need."

"Good idea." Wilson rose and came around the

desk to shake Jude's hand. "Good luck, Jude. Watch out for yourself."

Jude grinned and nodded. "I'll be fine." He turned and left, thinking about the names Wilson had mentioned. He'd never even met a real farmer, people who lived in houses made of sod. All he'd known was the Kingman mansion in north Chicago, one whole wing belonging just to him, with his own servants. He chuckled, imagining what his mother would think of women who lived on and helped work farms. Far be it from Corinne Kingman to actually touch dirt with her bare hands, to have even one hair out of place or ever to wear an apron.

Prim and proper, his mother was a respected philanthropist who perpetually found reasons to throw a fund-raiser dinner-dance so she could show off the third-floor ballroom of the family mansion and mingle with Chicago's finest. She was unmatched as a hostess, probably owned more jewels and clothes than any other high-society woman of Chicago, had recently raised money for a new library, was head of a Chicago historical society and attended church regularly. People thought she was wonderful.

Little did they know that Corinne Kingman had no idea how to be a mother, or that in his whole life Jude could not remember ever once being held close by her or ever once feeling loved by her. Only Mark had been privy to motherly attention.

As for being a regular at church, that was only an excuse for his mother to show off her newest hat or dress and pretend to be a proper and loving Christian woman. There were never any prayers at the table or any Bible readings in front of a fireplace, things he'd heard her tell others were a regular family tradition. The only thing he'd managed to garner from being forced to go to church for appearances' sake was to realize, somewhere in his own vague memory of things he'd heard preached, that something wasn't quite right about putting business and money ahead of hurting innocent people. Now he would be doing just that.

Chapter Four

Rain poured so hard that Ingrid and her father didn't hear a wagon pull up outside. Someone pounded on the door, and Albert jerked awake from an afternoon nap in his favorite wooden rocker near the fireplace. Ingrid looked up from her knitting as her father rose.

"I'll get it," he said, grimacing at the pain in his back as he stretched. He walked over and slid aside the wooden bar that kept the door tight. "It's Carl."

"Oh, my!" Ingrid set her knitting aside and hurried over to the stove. "I will heat some coffee." She knew the likely reason for Carl's visit, although he would come up with an excuse, probably the foul weather. Not long ago Carl had again talked to her father about marriage, which irritated her. Carl apparently took it for granted she would *want* to marry him. Good and hardworking as he was, the man didn't have an ounce of gentlemanly manners, or any idea how to properly court a woman.

Carl was ten years older than she, a huge man, at least six foot six, barrel-chested, loud and clumsy. Without a mother or any other woman around to teach him the gentle side of life, Carl was reared by a Swedish immigrant father who to this day barely spoke English, never having bothered to learn.

She removed a grate and stuffed some extra pieces of twisted corn husks inside the stove top where a few embers from breakfast quickly set fire to the fresh fuel. With hardly a tree in sight, corn husks or cobs and even dried buffalo chips or horse manure provided necessary fuel. All left a bigger mess than wood, but there was no other choice for heating and cooking.

"Vell, come in!" Albert greeted Carl in his own strong Swedish accent.

Ingrid replaced the grate and set what was left of the morning's coffee on the burner.

"Hello, my friend!" Carl answered. "Your porch

is dry, so I left my rubbers and my jacket there," he continued in a familiar singsong accent they all used. "I don't vant to get Ingrid's floors vet and muddy." The two men shook hands as Carl came inside. Johnny streaked out of his room to greet Carl.

"No running, Johnny," Ingrid reminded her brother. Her mind rushed on, wondering what to say to Carl. She'd not given the slightest hint that she even remotely cared to be his wife. Still, he visited often and paid no heed to her obvious lack of interest. Her father was no help. He liked Carl and encouraged her to see the man socially.

"Hello there, Ingrid!" Carl greeted her.

"Hello, Carl. I am surprised you came all the way here in such a downpour."

"Ah, vell, ve cannot do any vork, that's for sure," Carl answered in his booming voice.

"Ya, and I fear flooded fields," Albert told the man. "But then, I never mind an excuse to sit once in a while."

Both men laughed, and Ingrid smiled. For the next few minutes all three of them spoke Swedish, joined at times by Johnny, who'd been raised to know the language of his parents and ancestors. Still Ingrid knew it was important for her brother to speak good English, and she'd taught him as best she could, always practicing correct pronunciation herself. She'd learned from weekly trips to a tiny school at Plum Creek when she was younger. Albert had taken her there for lessons, insisting she learn "American" in every way. She was proud of how well she spoke English, her accent very subtle now. Johnny spoke even better English than she, having been born and raised in America.

Albert motioned for Carl to sit down at the wooden kitchen table, and then he and Johnny joined the man while Ingrid sliced some bread.

"I am vorried," Carl said, losing his smile.

Albert waved him off. "The rain vill make the ground easier to vork," he told Carl. "It vill stop soon, you'll see. Things vill be fine."

Carl shook his head. "It is not the rain that vorries me."

Ingrid set a wooden bowl of butter and some knives on the table, along with a plate of sliced bread.

"Then what is it that bothers you, Carl?" she asked, sitting down to join them, glad the conversation was not about her and marriage.

Johnny grabbed a piece of bread and began buttering it. "Have some, Carl. Ingrid makes real good butter."

Carl nodded. "Ah, yes, I vill have some of Ingrid's fine bread and butter." He beamed at Ingrid as he took a piece of bread, then sighed as he began buttering it. "It is the railroad that vorries me."

"And why is that?" Ingrid asked, alarmed at the worried look on Carl's face.

Carl finished buttering the bread and set it on a plate. "Vell, I vas in town two days ago, and the clerk at Hans Grooten's dry goods store told me that George Cain from the bank just came back from Omaha—big meeting there with other bankers about possibly losing money loaned to settlers on railroad land, because now the government says that land should not have been sold to us. He said crooked real estate men told us the land vas ours to settle and buy at cheap prices later on."

All grew silent for a moment as Ingrid and Albert pondered the statement.

"I do not understand," Albert said with a concerned frown.

"Nor do I," Carl answered. He bit into his bread and chewed for a moment. "The clerk, he said he thinks nothing is final yet, but this vorries me. After all our years of vork on this land, getting it to the shape it is in now, how can they come along and tell us it does not belong to us?"

A soft whistle from the coffeepot reminded Ingrid that the brew was warming. She rose to check it. "Surely that could never happen," she suggested, wanting to reassure not just Carl and Albert, but also herself. "What on earth would we do if someone came along and told us we had to get off this land? It is like a part of us." She turned back to face them. "Someone will come and tell us everything is just fine," she added. "Neither the railroad nor the government would do this to us."

She began pouring coffee into china cups, then set them on the table. She had to smile at how big and stubby Carl's fingers looked against the dainty cup as he lifted it. She actually worried that if he squeezed it too hard it would shatter in his hand.

Carl looked at her with big blue eyes, and again Ingrid felt guilty for not being able to find feelings for the blustery, loud man. He had a good heart and was a hardworking man who, anyone knew, would always provide for his family.

"I do not like the sound of it," Carl said after thanking Ingrid for the good coffee. "In this country the railroad is king. Ve all know that the government is owned by the railroad, and also the other vay around. If there is a legal problem, the railroad vill abide by what the government says because it is the government that gave them the land grants. There is big money involved here. This is a free country, yes, but it is run by the very rich. Do not forget that."

Although Ingrid was relieved that Carl's visit was not necessarily an excuse just to see her, she did not like the real reason he'd come. He was right about the railroad and the very rich. The two walked hand in hand.

"I think we should pray that these people are guided down the right path," she told her father and Carl.

"Praying for rich people does not alvays bring answers," Albert said despairingly. "The very rich are usually far from God and His vill."

"God works in his own ways, Far," Ingrid assured him. "A person's station in life means nothing to Him, and only He can change men's hearts. And we must remember that this land does not really belong to us, or to the railroad or even the government. It is God's land, loaned to us to care for and to provide food for us."

Carl scowled, and for the first time ever Ingrid saw a rather frightening anger in his eyes. "This might be God's land, but He chose us to love and care for it. He brought my father to America and led him here, and for many years my father and I have vorked it and slaved over the land. My mother is buried here, as is yours, Ingrid, and no man—no power of any kind—vill take my farm from me, and most of all not from my father. It vould *kill* him!"

Ingrid's heart went out to him. "Carl, don't let your anger get the better of you. You don't even know yet if anything will happen. It sounds like just a rumor right now."

Some of the anger left his eyes. "Perhaps. But..." He hesitated, softening even more, his face taking on a red glow. "Surely you know my feelings for you, Ingrid. My plan is someday to make you my beloved and raise our children on that farm."

Ingrid felt like crying from guilt. Why couldn't she love Carl? Was she a fool to keep turning him down? "Carl, I dearly appreciate your feelings and dreams, and I promise to think about them. But for now I have to think about Papa and Johnny. Apparently we need to wait and see if there will be trouble with the railroad. We all must pray and hope and go ahead with spring planting as always, as soon as weather permits. Promise me you will be patient and wise about your decisions if there is trouble. Do not do something foolish. This land has laws, and we must follow them."

Carl's normally bright eyes darkened again. "Ve shall see." He turned to Albert, who nodded in agreement.

"Ya. Maybe ve make our own laws."

Carl nodded.

"I will listen to no such talk, especially not in front of Johnny," Ingrid demanded.

Carl sighed, shaking his head. "I go now." He rose. "Ingrid, you think about what I told you. I am getting no younger, nor are you. A marriage could strengthen our cause against the railroad if that becomes necessary. Putting out a single man is one thing. Putting out a family is quite another, and ve could lay title to both farms if ve married."

What about love? Is that of only secondary importance? Ingrid wanted to ask. She turned away, pretending to check the Concord's ash pan. "Be careful going home in this rain, Carl." She heard him say his goodbyes to Albert and Johnny, heard the door open and close, then felt relieved he'd left.

She put her head in her hands. Relieved at his absence was not how a woman was supposed to feel about the man she might marry.

Chapter Five

Mid-May

Jude leaned to look out the window of his comfortable Pullman car as it rumbled into the unspectacular town of Plum Creek. The weather had warmed to seventy degrees, which would normally be comfortable. But he'd learned from other trips to Nebraska that the air here was often humid, as it was today, making the temperature seem warmer than it really was. Because of that, he'd lowered the windows on the railroad car, and the stench from a nearby pen of cattle wafted inside, causing him to choke on the air.

"Welcome to Plum Creek," he muttered. "Don't let the people here see you curling your nose at their town."

He leaned his head back for a moment, not relishing his reason for being here. As soon as the humble inhabitants of Plum Creek found out who he was and why he was here, they might forget their Christian background and be anything but welcoming.

With a sigh he rose and walked over to a huge, gold-framed mirror at one end of his parlor car where he adjusted his small bow tie, ran his hands through his thick hair and donned a black felt hat. It was Sunday. He figured he'd dress appropriately. People should be getting out of church about now, and most of them would be dressed up. It just seemed the thing to do on a Sunday. It had been a long time since he'd set foot in a church himself, but he pretty well knew what people expected on the Sabbath.

He straightened his shoulders and walked outside, standing on the car's platform as the behemoth steam engine farther ahead blared its whistle and let off huge bursts of steam, slowing gradually until the train stopped in front of the town's small depot. A few people wandered about, some probably expecting someone, or perhaps waiting for

supplies; others simply curious. Just as he'd figured, many were dressed up, and after a look at the
gold watch he pulled from his vest pocket, it became obvious most had indeed just come from
church. It was one o'clock..

A young man pointed toward his Pullman and
said something to another man about "Kingman
Enterprises." The second man answered something
about the railroad, and both ran off.

Here goes, Jude thought. Apparently the rumor
had already spread that someone from the railroad
might be paying the town a visit. Perhaps those
who'd run off were going for their guns. He smiled
grimly at the thought as he leaned against a support post, watching the usual bustle that ensued
when a train pulled into a depot.

Jude stayed on the platform of his car and simply watched. Plum Creek was not unlike every other
small town along the U.P.'s tracks from east to west.
There was the proverbial white church with a stee-
ple and a bell. He noticed a good deal of the people
approaching had come from there. Usually the farther west a person traveled, the more saloons the
towns sported. Since he saw only one in Plum Creek,
he gathered this was a very Christian town, although
that would indeed be put to the test when things became more heated over the reason he was here.

He noted a barbershop, a sheriff's office, a house with a sign that said Doctor, a lumber supply, three or four other supply stores, a livery, a blacksmith, a grocery store—all the usual businesses, plus a few which he could not see from where he stood.

The engine let off more steam, and children playing nearby screamed and laughed. Children loved steam engines. Fact was, so did grown men. He agreed they were certainly something to see, and he admitted to admiring their beastly qualities, the huge steel wheels, the very mightiness of a locomotive engine. There was something very masculine about a steam engine.

Well, what's this? he thought. He'd spotted something quite the opposite of masculine. She was as feminine as could be, and quite a sight for a lonely man's eyes. A young woman approached, with hair as bright as a hot yellow sun, and eyes as blue as the sky. Although the dress she wore was a far cry from designer-made, it fit her divine figure in ways that were pleasing to the eye. In spite of its plainness, and the fact that the woman obviously wore no special color on her face and no jewelry, she was beautiful. It struck him he'd never seen a woman so plain yet so lovely.

The three men who accompanied the woman

were as burly and rugged as the woman was beautiful and feminine. They were tall, light-haired, blue-eyed brutes who were obviously uncomfortable in their ill-made Sunday suits, men who were probably better suited to coveralls and pitchforks. No one could doubt they were farmers, especially from the way the sun had darkened and toughened their fair skin. Jude actually found himself feeling grateful that the woman with them showed little sign of sun-induced aging. She probably had sense enough to wear a wide-brimmed bonnet when out of doors, although today she wore a simple straw hat decorated with a few blue silk flowers.

He couldn't help noticing the four of them, since they marched close to his Pullman, the three men showing obvious scorn at the sight of the car and its passenger. The woman, on the other hand, appeared more curious than angry, and since Jude had grown accustomed to young women fawning over him, he actually felt disappointment that this particular young woman showed no such interest. He gave her his most charming smile, and she immediately took on a look of wariness, accompanied by a bit of an air, her chin rising slightly, determined contempt coming into those amazing blue eyes. Two of the men with her appeared older, more fatherly, but one was younger, and that one stepped closer then, an obvious challenge in his eyes.

"Who are you, mister? You look like one of them fancy railroad men. Ve don't vant *no* railroad men coming here!"

Jude guessed he was probably the woman's brother or, heaven forbid, her husband. To think that she might have a husband greatly disturbed Jude, and then he realized how absurd it was to care. Because she wore gloves he couldn't see her left hand. The younger man stood there with his fists clenched at his side, so Jude couldn't see his left hand, either. Then again, maybe big, rugged Swedish farmers didn't wear wedding rings. Deducing that the man was Swedish was quite simple, considering the easily discernible accent in the few short words he'd spoken.

"It might be nice to have a chance to introduce myself and be welcomed into your town," Jude told him.

"Ve don't velcome thieves in Plum Creek," the big Swede answered.

"Yeah!"

"That's right!"

More men had gathered and were backing up the Swede.

"You people don't even know who I am or why

I'm here," Jude told them. Clearly, this job was going to be much harder than he'd thought. He hadn't even set foot on solid ground in Plum Creek, yet these people were ready to ride him right back out.

"Carl, we just left church, for goodness' sake," the lovely young woman told the Swede. "Where are your manners?"

Good for you, Jude thought. *She's no withering flower.* "Yes, Carl, where are your manners?" he spoke aloud, now that he'd heard the man's name.

"Don't need manners around the likes of you. Ve have heard a railroad man vas coming here to tell us ve must get off our farms. It is illegal! If you are the one come to tell us, go avay!"

Now even more people gathered. Jude eyed the young blond woman, who looked apologetic. A young boy of perhaps nine or ten ran up to her then, and Jude's hopes fell. Though she looked too young, she must be the boy's mother, which meant the big Swede was probably her husband. Now, why in the world did that disappoint him?

More voices were raised, and Jude put up his hands to silence them. "Look, everyone, my name is Jude Kingman, of Kingman Enterprises in Chicago. And yes, I am here to talk to some of you about your farms, but don't go getting all excited and defensive. I'll be here throughout the summer, and I am not here to tell you that you can't plant and harvest your crops this year. Just go ahead and work your farms as you would any other time. I assure you I am only here to look things over and study the problems that might arise over a land issue with the railroad—and that I fully intend to find a way to absolve those problems without huge losses to anyone."

"Fancy talk! That's all you're about!" another man shouted. "Go on back to Chicago!"

The blond-haired woman appeared completely exasperated with all of them. Glancing angrily at the big Swede, she turned to the young boy and grabbed his arm, walking off with him. Jude was actually disappointed he'd not got her name.

"I'm not leaving anytime soon," Jude told the crowd. "I will probably make my railroad parlor car into an office while I'm here, and gradually I will be coming out to visit some of you on your farms—just to talk. Any of you are welcome to come and see me whenever I'm in town. I fully intend to hear your side of this matter and do my best to keep the peace." He glanced around at all of them, an intimidating crowd indeed, made up of big, tough farmers and stern women who could probably hold their own against any of the men.

"You'll talk to us, all right," another man shouted,

"then ignore everything we tell you and stab us in the back! Anybody can see you're a rich man come here to do a rich man's business, which is to walk all over the poor, so don't be telling us lies about why you're here."

"I am not a liar, sir," Jude answered. "I assure you, I have only the best of intentions, and I will be far more open to your needs than some of the other men who might have been sent here for the job. Don't waste an opportunity to possibly save your farms."

"There! You see?" the big Swede shouted. "He is already talking about saving our farms. You know what that means!"

"Yeah!"

"Yeah!"

"Is this how you always greet strangers in Plum Creek?" Jude shouted above them. He refused to show any sign of intimidation. "Perhaps I'd be better off talking with your sheriff and perhaps your town preacher. They might know a little more about how you should be conducting yourselves. I've not said one word about coming here to do you harm, nor have I been so rude and unwelcoming as all of you have been toward me. One would think I'd come here packing six-guns and a whip! I believe a good many of you walked over here from Sunday church services. Is this what God teaches about welcoming strangers?"

A few of them took on rather sheepish looks.

"I will hold town meetings as soon as I can get things organized," Jude added then, keeping his voice raised. "I will be every bit a gentleman and I expect the same from good, Christian people like yourselves."

He waited, hoping his talent for exuding charm and saying the right words when necessary would calm them. A few of the women stared, and he smiled and nodded toward them. Some blushed and covered their mouths as they quietly laughed, others just scowled and turned away. Some of the men seemed to change their initial feelings of anger and defense. They mumbled among themselves, and a couple of them actually apologized, saying they would be willing to listen but were not about to hand over their land to anyone. Jude assured them that no one was asking them to do so.

The big Swede never changed his attitude. He glowered at Jude a moment longer, then turned to the two older men who'd accompanied him. "Come on. Ve got supplies to get," he said, stalking off with them.

Jude decided he'd better stay inside his private car for a while. He might be better off this first day waiting until most of the farmers had left with their supplies before exiting the Pullman to explore Plum Creek. He rubbed the back of his neck, feeling a headache coming on.

Thank you, Dad, for giving me this glorious job, he thought wryly.

He turned to go back inside, but then he caught sight of the young boy he'd seen earlier with the pretty blond woman. The kid had apparently run back to see what was going on. He waved at Jude, and Jude nodded to him. The blond woman came around the corner of the depot then, spotting the boy and hurrying over to scold him for coming back after she'd told him not to. She glanced at Jude, and all Jude could think was... Oh, my!

He tipped his hat to the woman and gave her a smile.

"I am sorry for the way you were treated," she told him in good English, although there was a slight Swedish lilt to the words.

He bowed slightly. "Apology accepted, ma'am."

She hurried away with the young boy, and again Jude chastised himself for not getting her name or doing his best to find out how she was related to the three men with her earlier.

He went inside his Pullman, shaking his head at his own ridiculous reaction to the blond woman.

If she was a friend of, or related to the big Swede who'd been so rude to him, there was a good chance he'd see her again once he started visiting the farmers. He decided to go over the list Wilson had given him and see if he could figure out who she might be.

He threw his hat to the other end of the car and yelled for the butler he'd brought along to bring him a cool drink. He sat down in a plush velvet chair and kicked off his shoes, leaning his head back and groaning over the hideous job his father had given him. He could already see that this was going to be one long, hot summer.

Chapter Six

Ingrid stopped midrow and set down her gunny sack of corn kernels. She put a hand to the small of her back, stretching backward, then rolled her head forward and to the side, stretching her neck. Every fiber of her being screamed for rest, but planting time did not allow it. The only thing that mattered was temperature and weather, and the ideal time to plant.

Such was the life of a Nebraska farmer, along with a lot of praying that this year the grasshoppers would feast someplace else. But there was a positive side to both planting and harvesting. For both events, area farmers got together and helped one another, and for the past three days Carl and Stanley Unger had been on her farm with plows and horses. After making furrows, Ingrid, Johnny and Ingrid's father followed, dropping kernels into the long trenches. Now, Carl and Stanley followed the planters with hoes, covering the kernels. The only thing left was to pray for just the right amount of rain and sunshine so that the harvest would be plentiful, with enough corn to store for their own use and plenty more to sell to buyers in Plum Creek.

She breathed deeply of the fresh, cool air. Since the downpours earlier in the month had ended, the weather had remained accommodating. She watched Carl and Stanley, again thinking what a fool she probably was for not committing herself to the strong and faithful Carl. He was not extremely handsome, but certainly decent looking, plain but stalwart.

"When will we be done?" Johnny asked with a pout, his face sunburned.

"You just asked me that five minutes ago," Ingrid answered, shaking her head. "Just keep planting. The time will go faster than you think."

Johnny frowned with impatience and rather reluctantly continued dropping corn into the furrows. Ingrid dipped her hand into her gunny sack, then noticed a carriage approaching along the narrow dirt road that led from Plum Creek to the farm. From what she could tell, the rig appeared to be fancier than any local visitor would use.

"Who on earth would bother us during planting time?" she muttered, irritated. Stopping now would upset the rhythm of plowing, sowing and covering the rows. She shouted to her father that someone was coming.

"This is no time for visiting!" her father yelled in reply, obviously annoyed. "Go see vat they vant, Ingrid. Then you might as vell quit and start supper."

Ingrid shaded her eyes to see the buggy fast approaching, and she felt suddenly self-conscious of her appearance. Their visitor was indeed most likely. a buyer, which meant it was a man of some importance from the city, and here she was a mess, her hands dirty from earth and kernel dust, her homespun dress stained, her hair falling from its bun.

She untied her slat bonnet as she hastily made her way between two furrows, hurrying as best she could in the loose dirt, feeling a little upset that a buyer, someone who should know better, had the audacity to come here during planting. More of her hair fell loose during the nearly ten minutes it took her to make her way back to the house. On the way she could see that their visitor had indeed arrived in a very handsome rig, pulled by a magnificently groomed black gelding wearing blinders. The rig was driven by a rather burly man wearing a plain brown tweed jacket and a brown felt hat. Beside him sat...

"Oh, my goodness," Ingrid muttered. It was the railroad man, Jude Kingman. Her heart sank as she guessed the purpose of his visit.

The driver pulled at the reins to halt the handsome horse, and Jude Kingman climbed down. A gold watch chain hung from the pocket of his pale blue-and-black patterned vest, over which the strikingly handsome man wore a well-tailored, deep gray topcoat with black velvet lapels and black pipe trim.

Ingrid slowed her approach, feeling apprehensive, angry, yet slightly taken aback by her visitor's dashing appearance. She hadn't forgotten his stunning looks since seeing him two weeks ago at the train depot. He came closer and removed his hat, bowing slightly, then smiled...and oh, what a smile! His teeth were straight and amazingly white. His brown eyes were outlined with dark brows, and his straight nose was centered above a neatly trimmed mustache, full lips and a square-cut jawline. Thick, dark hair showed from the sides of his hat.

For some reason her visitor seemed somewhat surprised at the sight of her, and also pleased. He briefly adjusted a string tie at the neck of his white ruffled shirt before speaking.

"Well, if it isn't the lovely woman I saw at the train depot! What a pleasant surprise. You must be Miss Ingrid Svensson. My records tell me that's who lives here." He looked past her at the men working in the field as though he didn't quite trust them.

More conscious than ever of her appearance, Ingrid pushed a piece of hair behind her ear. "Yes, I am Ingrid." She stood there feeling plain and embarrassed. "Please excuse my appearance, but we are planting today."

Kingman looked her over as though she were not a mess at all, but rather something quite agreeable to the eye. "No excuses necessary," he answered. "Your beauty overcomes the situation."

Rogue! He was a smooth talker, this one. "I remember you, Mr. Kingman, also from that day at the depot. And I assure you, flattery will not help your cause." Still, his smile seemed so genuine.

"Ma'am, my compliment was just a statement of fact, not a ruse to win your favor." He looked around. "You have a nice farm here—well kept."

"Thank you, but you have picked a poor time to talk about the farm. We do not stop planting to visit *or* to talk business, especially when the weather is as perfect as it has been lately. And now I have supper to fix. If you are here to discuss business, I suggest that you leave and come back in ten days or so. Better yet, do not come back at all, as we have nothing to talk about."

Kingman's eyebrows shot up in apparent dismay at her stance. "Ma'am, I admire your directness."

Ingrid put her hands on her hips. "As you said a moment ago, Mr. Kingman, it's just a statement of fact. I do apologize for the rude treatment you received at the railroad depot, but if you do not leave this minute, it could happen again. You are obviously not a welcome sight to farmers." She glanced back at her father and Carl. "Please, do go now. I want no trouble on my land, and there will be trouble if my father and Mr. Unger realize who is here."

Kingman seemed unfazed. "I do apologize for coming at such a busy time," he told her, "but I truly am here just to look around. In the business world we, too, have schedules to keep. I'm just doing my job the same as you and your family and friends are doing, Miss Svensson."

"Oh? And just what is that job, Mr. Kingman? To kick us out? I see you brought a gunman with you."

He glanced at his man still in the buggy. "Benjamin is just a bodyguard. After that somewhat doubtful reception at Plum Creek, I thought it wise to have a little backup along when I visit you farmers." He looked toward the fields again. "But then your father should be present when we talk, and apparently he's not about to come in from the fields. I can certainly understand why on such a busy day."

"If you knew anything about farming and hard work, Mr. Kingman, you would not have picked this time to come here in the first place."

Kingman frowned. "I can assure you, ma'am, that I do understand hard work. I express my deepest apologies for disturbing you at this time. I am just out taking a look at the various farms on railroad property, getting to know the owners and getting an idea of the situation as a whole."

Ingrid folded her arms. "The situation? What situation is that, Mr. Kingman? Would it be whether or not we should be ordered off of our own land? Would it be wondering if some farmers will fight you? I can assure you, they will, and I do not look forward to the strife your presence will cause for Plum Creek."

Kingman put his hands to his waist. "I thought you were too busy to talk about these things."

Ingrid closed her eyes and drew a deep breath.

"If talking about them is inevitable, then you may come back in two weeks, but be assured that if you are coming to tell us this is not our land, it is a fruitless trip on your part. This land is ours by right, for the simple fact that we have worked it for nine years now, longer than the transcontinental railroad has even existed, on land promised us *by* the railroad so that more people would settle out here and in turn *use* that railroad. So since you are such a busy man, Mr. Kingman, do not waste your time on small farmers like us."

Ingrid turned to leave, and it was then she noticed Carl walking toward them. "Oh, dear!" she muttered. She turned back to her visitor. "Please, go *now*!" she told him. "The man walking toward us has a temper, let alone the fact that he is tired and will be very irritated to know it's you who has interrupted this very important work. If you expect any kind of decent conversation with any of us, come back at a better time! I am telling you for your own good."

Something about the way Mr. Kingman looked at her then seemed to open a window to the inner man, an odd spark of sympathy and understanding, something she would not have expected from a man of his wealth and power, a man she'd guessed had no concern at all for people "beneath" him. He tipped his hat again. "As you wish. I only came to meet you and look the place over, nothing more."

"Hey! Who are you? Vat do you vant? Ve are busy here!"

Kingman looked Ingrid over again. "You know, ma'am, in spite of the condition you are in right now, I feel compelled to tell you that you are one of the most beautiful women I've ever set eyes on."

Leaving Ingrid rather stunned by the remark, he turned and headed back to the carriage. His bodyguard started to climb down when he saw Carl approaching, but Kingman ordered him to take it easy. "I want no trouble," Ingrid heard him say.

"Vait up there!" Carl yelled. "You that man from the railroad? Vait there and I vill show you vat ve think of people who cheat others and rob from them!"

Ingrid turned. "Carl!" She reached out and grabbed his arm just as he got close enough. By then Jude Kingman was in the carriage seat. His bodyguard snapped the reins, urging the beautiful black horse into a modest trot.

"That vas that fancy railroad man, ya?" Carl demanded of Ingrid.

Ingrid stared after the carriage as she answered. "Ya."

"Did he say vat he vanted?"

She finally turned and faced Carl, struck by the stark contrast between him and Jude Kingman. "You already know what he wanted. He said he was here to look over farms that are on railroad land and to meet the owners. I told him he'd come at a very poor time and that he should wait a couple of weeks before coming back."

"Ya, vell he had better not come back at all! If he shows up at *my* place, he might not leave standing up!"

"Carl Unger, you stop that kind of talk! Nothing is worth committing violence against another man!"

"Nothing? I am not so sure." Carl turned and walked off to finish his share of the planting. Ingrid turned and watched the buggy disappear over a low rise, heading toward Plum Creek. She put a hand to her heart, feeling guilty that although she was upset over the likely reason for Jude Kingman's visit, he'd left quite an impression.

Shame on you, Ingrid Svensson! she told herself. *The man is after your* farm *of all things!* She marched into the house to prepare supper, hoping against hope that "that railroad man" would not come back at all.

Chapter Seven

Mid-June

Still irritated at the intrusion on his time and work, Jude disembarked his private Pullman after it pulled into the Omaha train yard. He had no trouble spotting his mother's extravagantly decorated private cars attached to a nearby train. Gold trim accented her "home on wheels," a sleeper car, dining car and also a lounge car for receiving visitors. Along the edge of the rounded rooftops was the name Union Pacific in small letters. The words, Kingman Enterprises, however, were written in much bigger and fancier gold letters on the sides of the cars.

A young woman whom Jude recognized as one of his mother's personal servants gingerly made her way across several tracks that lay between the two trains. She spotted Jude and then yelled above the roar of a burst of steam from a nearby engine.

"Mrs. Kingman is in her private car just over there," she said, pointing. "She's been waiting for you, sir."

Yes, let's not keep Her Highness waiting, Jude thought. He climbed down from his own Pullman, wondering what on earth was so important that his mother had come clear down here from Chicago to talk to him. Far be it from her to conveniently meet him in Plum Creek or at his railroad office here in Omaha. Mrs. Jefferson Kingman wouldn't be caught dead setting foot in a town she considered inferior to her standards, let alone get dust on the hem of one of her expensive dresses.

Jude dreaded one-on-one visits with Corinne, which was how he thought of her most of the time, a woman named Corinne, not his mother. It irked him that she could still stir emotions in him only a younger child should have—the hurt of feeling unworthy, unloved and unwanted. He steeled himself against her hard, dark eyes before he even climbed up the platform to her car.

The door opened before he could knock, and there stood the woman he seldom saw. They both led such busy lives in different ways, and there was no closeness between them to warrant going out of their way to see each other, which made this visit all the more odd. Even when they were all home at the sprawling Kingman mansion, they seldom ran into each other or dined together.

And, of course, there was that look—not a "glad to see you, son" look, but more like "it's about time you got here." Corinne was accustomed to snapping her fingers or ringing a bell and receiving almost instant gratification.

"Come in quickly," she said curtly. "The train yard here smells of cattle, and I'm trying to keep the odor out of this car."

Jude walked inside the richly carpeted train car. Heavy velvet curtains at the windows kept it so dark that light had to be provided with small gaslights on the walls. "It's hot in here," he complained. "I'd rather smell cattle than sweat to death."

"I will open the windows when I leave, which will be soon," his mother answered, turning to walk to a satin-covered chair. "Your father doesn't even know I am here," she said, sitting down. "I told him I was going to see my sister in St. Louis."

Jude folded his arms. "Well, I'm glad to see you, too, Mother. May I sit down?"

"Of course, Jude. Don't be silly." She suddenly softened somewhat, but Jude knew the woman well. Her moods could change in an instant, and usually were designed to get whatever she wanted. "I'm sorry to take you from your work," she added.

He didn't believe that. He sat down in a chair across from her, removing his hat and taking a handkerchief from a vest pocket to dab at perspiration on his forehead. "You *should* be sorry. I had to take a train all the way back here from Plum Creek, and on a Sunday, which is the best day to be in town to talk to settlers. A lot of them come into town on Sundays for church and to buy supplies."

Corinne, too, dabbed at perspiration with a lace handkerchief. "I can't imagine having to stay in that horrible little town. There isn't even a decent hotel here in Omaha, let alone a little farm town like Plum Creek." She sniffed. "What a quaint name."

Jude noticed that in spite of the heat, her form-fitting dress was tidy and unwrinkled. Every one of her graying hairs was in place, a jeweled comb perfectly positioned in sausage curls on top of her head. His mother was still beautiful and slender—

too thin, actually. She was like a piece of china that might break if touched the wrong way.

"Plum Creek isn't that bad," he answered. "Besides, I stay in my Pullman, just like you do in such places, although I am establishing an office there." Jude leaned forward, resting his elbows on his knees. "Now, why don't you tell me why you're here? You'd never come to Omaha just to visit. And what's wrong with Dad knowing about this?"

Corinne fussed with the lace trim on her dress. "Because he doesn't like it when I come between him and his decisions, especially when it involves you and Mark."

Jude understood immediately. His mother would never come here just to see *him,* but she'd probably go to Plum Creek herself and dig in the dirt with the farmers if it meant doing something to help *Mark.* "I should have known this had something to do with my brother, although I can't imagine what it is."

Corinne stiffened and raised her chin. "Jude, dear..." She hesitated.

Jude almost laughed. *Dear?* The woman must be ready to beg!

"I know about the job your father has given you. However..."

Her hesitation made Jude wary. "However

what?" He felt his anger building, imagining how nice it would have been if she'd really come here just to see him—as any normal mother would do. He saw her put on her authoritative demeanor then.

"Mark came to me about this—this assignment, or whatever you want to call it. He's very upset that your father gave you this job. Mark feels it should have gone to him, in spite of how much he'd hate going to a place like Plum Creek. You've been here a month already, and hardly anything has been accomplished, according to Mark. He wants the chance to prove to his father that he can do better in a situation like this. I came to ask—well—I just wish you'd go back to Chicago and tell your father you've decided you can't do this and that Mark is the better one for the job."

For a moment Jude just stared at her, dumbfounded. Then he shook his head. "You know, Mother, I've always known you favored Mark and that he could get anything he wanted out of you, but to go crying to you at his age about this—it's like a little kid begging his mother to let him have a certain toy instead of his brother."

"Don't insult him! He doesn't even know I am here. He simply complained to me about it, that's all."

Jude snickered. "Do you know how ridiculous

your request is? I'm not going back to Chicago like some whining child and ask Daddy dear to please not make me do this. Besides, Dad knows what Mark can do. Personally I don't think he *is* the right one for the job, because he would use tactics that would only enrage the farmers and cause possible riots and damage to the railroad and who knows what else? I have some ideas I am trying to utilize to make this all happen peacefully and without making the Kingman name look bad. That's why it's taking some time. So you can go back to Chicago and tell Mark to get to work on the things he's *supposed* to be doing!" He rose. "I've really enjoyed our visit, Mother. I hate to cut things short, but I have to get back to Plum Creek."

"Jude, just think about it, will you? Mark is anxious to come down here and take care of this."

Jude studied her eyes. "You know, Mother, I'd really like to know what I've ever done to make you so prejudiced toward Mark. I graduated with top honors from Yale, far better grades, I might add, than Mark ever got. On top of that, I'm your firstborn son."

There it was, that way she had of looking away slightly when he talked about being her son. Then she stiffened again as she rose. "That's just it. You outdo poor Mark in everything. You're bigger and far more handsome and young women beg for your hand, while Mark…" She peered at him intently. "The reason your father doesn't give you the important jobs is because Mark needs to feel important. He needs the confidence it gives him to know he can handle anything Kingman Enterprises might expect of him, and your father recognizes that Mark has that slight ruthlessness that it takes to run a business as big as your father's." She seemed to plead with him again. "Why can't you just marry into one of the wealthy families of Chicago and settle down and quietly do what's expected of you and let Mark have more of the limelight?"

Jude walked past her. "I haven't found one woman among our family's snobby friends worth marrying. And I *am* doing what is expected of me. I'm the one Dad sent down here, remember?" He walked toward the door again. "I have to say, Mother, that if I'd known Mark wanted this glorious assignment, I'd have gladly given it to him. But until Dad tells me differently, I'll do it myself and I'll do it my way. Now, why don't you have the engineer find out how soon you can get going on down to St. Louis to see dear Aunt Flo?" He opened the door, studying her pleading eyes for a moment, wondering if she'd ever once in her life been so terribly concerned about him instead of Mark, and then he walked out.

He picked his way over railroad tracks and to the engineer of the train that had brought him here. "Get me back to Plum Creek as soon as possible!" he ordered.

"Yes, sir."

Jude stormed inside his own Pullman, not even glancing back at his mother's car. The woman was losing her mind. And her talk of marriage... Did she really think that would solve anything? How could he marry when he might end up with someone like his own mother? What a great life that would be! It would serve her right if he married some farm girl from Plum Creek. That would certainly wilt the feathers in her hat!

He slammed the door and opened every window in the car. Stink or not, he needed air. Fact was, he'd been around the smell of cattle and farming so long now that he was getting used to the pungent odor. The factory smells in Chicago weren't much better.

He sat down with deliberate force, angry over the entire railroad matter. For some reason Ingrid Svensson came to mind then, probably because he'd intended to go and pay her that second visit today, until he'd got the telegram from his mother yesterday afternoon. He realized that was what he was most upset about. He'd actually been looking forward to going back out to see Miss Svensson. He'd meant it when he'd told her she was beautiful, in spite of all that dirt and that plain dress and her disheveled hair. He'd been so pleased to learn that the beautiful woman he'd first seen at the railroad depot was "Miss" Ingrid Svensson rather than a "Mrs."

What a stark contrast a woman like Ingrid was to his mother, or any of the young women he knew back in Chicago. She wasn't just more beautiful in looks. She was more beautiful in spirit and fortitude, stronger, more independent. From that one visit he could tell the woman didn't have an ounce of vanity, but a lot of courage and pride. He was actually looking forward to seeing her again, in a way he'd never anticipated seeing any young woman he'd dated in Chicago.

Chapter Eight

Early July

Ingrid and Johnny walked each row of corn, the eighteen-inch stalks tall enough to begin watching for corn borers. Each time Ingrid spotted a damaging bug or worm, she picked it off. Johnny held out a jar of kerosene and in the bug went, never to fly or eat again.

"So far it all looks good," Ingrid commented.

Johnny grinned. "Far says if we get in a good crop, we might be able to buy our land from the railroad if we have to."

Ingrid sobered, irritated that she'd lost many a night's sleep since Jude Kingman's visit. He'd not come back yet, which was fine with her, but a few other farmers had already received eviction notices, effective November first. That gave them barely enough time to know what their profits would be from the corn harvest.

Carl and Stanley Unger were already working hard at establishing a branch of the National Grange at Plum Creek, deciding there was power in numbers. Farmers were gathering together in protest over their treatment by the railroad, unfair pricing and the tyrannical attitude of the Union Pacific. Ingrid could see the deep unrest that was building to anger and very un-Christian behavior.

So far she'd convinced her father not to join the Grangers. She worried that could bring more trouble than it was worth. She'd heard rumors of destroying railroad property, and a few men, including Carl, talked of using guns to keep railroad men off their land. She hated Johnny hearing such talk.

Carl was beginning to show a side to his personality that gave her even more doubt about whether she wanted to marry the man. A few days ago he'd visited them to rant and rave about a neighboring German farmer, Vernon Krueger, who'd already given up his farm and was now working for the railroad. He called Vernon a money-hungry, penny-pinching, cowardly traitor, and the sight of Carl's clenched fists haunted Ingrid.

To make matters worse, Ingrid felt pressured by both her father's and Carl's talk of how a marriage could ensure that at least one of the farms would be saved. Combining their profits this fall might leave them money to hire help, since Ingrid's father's back was getting no better. Perhaps they could buy one of the farms and live on it as one family.

What upset Ingrid the most was Carl's suggestion she could "cook and clean for his father, too." There was nothing romantic about his suggestion. It sounded more as though she was being bartered for a railroad deal and would be nothing more than a servant. Marriage to Carl seemed more and more like a business deal than an act of love.

God, forgive my thoughts. Help me to know what to do. The womanly side of her wanted love and gentleness and sweet words. Her practical side told her Carl was right. Marriage could solve their railroad problem as well as bring her father the relief he needed from hard work, maybe even prolong his life. And there was Johnny to think about.

"Hey, somebody is coming," Johnny told her

then, interrupting her thoughts. "Looks like that fancy buggy again."

Ingrid looked toward the house, and against all that was right, her heartbeat quickened when she recognized the approaching buggy.

"Stay here, Johnny, and keep picking off worms." She lamented that, again, she was not presentable for company, especially the likes of Jude Kingman. This time she was not only dirty and wearing a plain, gray, homespun dress, but she also smelled of kerosene. "So be it," she told herself as she walked toward the house.

Why should she worry about how she looked to a total stranger who was here to steal her farm? Never once had she worried about how she looked when Carl came calling. She drew a deep breath, steeling herself to go head-to-head with Kingman. By the time she reached her soddy, the debonair man was already standing on the porch waiting for her. She deliberately gave him a look of cool greeting.

"I would say welcome, Mr. Kingman, if only I thought you were here for a good reason." She glanced at his carriage. "Where is your gunman?"

Kingman removed a black felt hat. "Other than my driver, I came alone, ma'am," he said, bowing.

Oh, but aren't you smooth, Mr. Kingman, she

thought. Today he looked as elegant as the first time he'd visited. He wore a neat black suit with a silver satin vest under his jacket, and his dashing looks made it difficult for a young woman to be rude.

"Sit down, Mr. Kingman," she said with a sigh of resignation. "My father is at Carl Unger's farm, which is probably just as well. Carl Unger is prepared to shoot you if you show up at his place. We have time to talk. I have as much say in what happens to this farm as he does." She brushed at her dress. "Forgive my condition, but yet again you have come on a very busy day. That is the life on a farm in summertime."

Kingman looked her over. "Miss Svensson, I can't imagine you being in any condition that could possibly hide your beauty. Never apologize for how you look. If you knew anything about me and some of the people I know, you'd realize that the way you look is absolutely refreshing to me."

Ingrid frowned. "Am I amusing you, Mr. Kingman?"

He lost his smile and looked completely serious. "No, ma'am. I am definitely not laughing at you. I am admiring you." He glanced at the soddy, curiosity in his eyes. "I've never seen a house like this. Can I look inside?"

A bit confused and wary, Ingrid opened the door. "Be my guest, Mr. Kingman." Now she was the one who wanted to laugh. The man seemed utterly fascinated with the soddy. She followed him inside and waited while he took a look around. She couldn't help wondering what he thought of the dirt walls and mostly handmade furniture. The braided oval rug in the center of the main room was also handmade.

"You have a very nice little house here, Miss Svensson," he told her, turning. "I never knew these places could be so pleasant and cool."

"My father and neighbors built it with their own hands, which is one of the reasons it would break our hearts to have to leave it," she answered with a warning look. "Come back outside and we'll sit on the porch and talk. Would you like some coffee?"

He nodded. "That would be very nice. And what is that wonderful smell?"

Ingrid felt compelled to be pleasant to the man, as he was behaving so gentlemanly. "It is either the rising bread dough that you smell—" she held up her hands "—or the kerosene on my hands."

Kingman laughed, and she groaned inwardly. What had made her joke with this man? He walked back outside, and Ingrid poured some still-warm coffee into two china cups and carried them out, then handed one to Jude. She sat down in a nearby chair, girding herself for whatever was to come.

"I am sure you are accustomed to being served in some fancier way, Mr. Kingman, but this is the best I can do. This china came all the way from Sweden. It was my grandmother's."

"I'm surprised it made it all the way across the ocean and clear out here to Nebraska in one piece." Kingman studied the cup. "It's exquisite—as fine as I've seen."

"Thank you. It is lovely, isn't it? It was packed in straw all the way here. My mother was over-joyed when she discovered none had broken. I remember the smile on her face." She sipped some coffee. "I miss my mother. She died when my brother was born." She met Kingman's eyes. "Is your mother still alive, Mr. Kingman?"

He took another drink of coffee. "Yes," he answered rather blandly, apparently having nothing more to say about the woman.

"Then you are a lucky man."

He cast her an odd look of doubt. "Some might say so." Before Ingrid could comment he quickly changed the subject. "I don't suppose any of that wonderful-smelling bread is already baked?"

"No, but if you wish I could hurry and bake some for you. The dough only needs to rise a few more minutes. I don't suppose I could buy you off with fresh loaves of bread?"

Her comment brought more laughter. What was it about the man that made her feel rather easy with him in spite of his occupation and the reason he was here, let alone his social standing? He seemed the epitome of the wealthy American businessman about whom she'd heard stories, people like the Vanderbilts.

"I just might consider that offer," he told her. He looked at her with sincere appreciation in his eyes. "You know what I like about you, Miss Svensson? There is nothing pretentious about you."

Ingrid found herself blushing. "I don't even know what that means," she admitted, then immediately wished she hadn't.

He chuckled, and Ingrid wondered if he was laughing at her. "It means you are genuine—you don't put on airs and pretend to be something you're not."

Was the man being "pretentious" himself, handing out compliments because he wanted her cooperation? "Perhaps we should quit all this small talk and discuss why you are *really* here," she told him, "although I think I already know. You're here to tell me to get off this land or buy it. I will not do the first, but I can try to do the second. The problem is, forcing us to buy this land for far more than we were originally promised is like coming here with your gunman and asking me to hand over my purse. It is robbery, Mr. Kingman, plain and simple."

He drank more coffee before answering. "I'm sorry you see it that way." He studied her with dark eyes, his smile gone. "Truly I am. All I can say, ma'am, is that in spite of all the help we've received from the government, the railroad is still nearly broke. There are still not enough people out here and farther west to support railroad expenses, which is why we have to ask such high prices to travel by rail. That in turn keeps business down, so we're caught in a vicious circle. We either ask for more money for the land the government granted us, or we sell it to the highest bidder. If we can do that, we can also lower our prices for passengers, which will in turn encourage more settlement farther west. When towns along the railroad grow and more industry and business come west and— well, I think you get the picture. It all starts with the proper use of the government land grants."

"And what about people like you, Mr. Kingman? What are the railroad builders and executives giving up to help out? I heard from a member of the Grangers that some of you used your own steel businesses and your own construction contractors to build the railroad in the first place, so whatever the government paid toward that construction went right back into your pockets. And of course you charged outrageous prices to fatten the purse even more. And you took advantage of all those Chinese people and other foreigners at rock-bottom wages, so labor certainly was not a big cost. How will *you* help out, Mr. Kingman?"

He leaned forward, his elbows resting on his knees. "*This* is my sacrifice, Miss Svensson. I've been given the dubious honor of telling people like you that it's either pay up or leave, and I hate it."

Why was she happy to hear him say that? "Then turn down the job."

He looked at her as though he thought her remark ridiculous. "Miss Svensson, if I sat here and told you my reasons for doing this…" He shook his head. "Miss, my own father sent me out here, and if you knew Jefferson Kingman—"

"There is only one Father, sir, and we should think of pleasing Him above all else. If your earthly father has asked you to do something you know is basically wrong, then you should do what pleases your heavenly Father."

Kingman smiled and shook his head. "I'm afraid I don't know much about that Father," he answered.

"I find that very sad, Mr. Kingman."

He frowned and set his coffee cup on the porch railing. "Now, look, Miss Svensson, we are getting off the subject of this visit. Yes, a lot of men benefited from the railroad through graft and dealings under the table. I feel the same way you do about that, but many of those investors were also men who saw that the railroad could do more to unite this country and make it stronger than anything else that's come along. Since we're still recovering from an ugly civil war, that union is more important than ever. I'm sorry that it's come to this, but now we need to make sure railroad land is properly utilized. I know I keep repeating myself, but what's done is done, and what must be, must be."

Ingrid slowly nodded. "Good speech, Mr. Kingman. I am sure you are accustomed to giving public talks, and to telling other businessmen what they want to hear in order to close deals. Perhaps what you just said was genuine, but even so, our hearts are in this farm. Far and I dream of my little brother owning it some day. Tell me, Mr. Kingman, did you have to work and sacrifice and earn and build all that you have today, or was it all handed to you by your father?" She actually saw a look of sadness in his eyes and caught herself. "I'm sorry. That was a rude remark. It's not like me to—"

"People come from all walks of life," he interrupted. "I can't help what I was born into any more than you can, Miss Svensson." He leaned back and sighed. "We aren't always handed what we want in life, and contrary to what you might think, my life isn't all that wonderful, at least not when it comes to personal matters." He looked suddenly embarrassed. "I have no idea why I told you that." He reached into a pocket inside his jacket and handed her a folded piece of paper. "That's a legal document, telling you that if you can't pay the required price for your land, which is three hundred dollars per acre, by November first, you will have to vacate this property. I'm sorry, but I have no choice but to give you this."

He rose rather wearily, as though burdened. Then after picking up his hat from where he'd set it on the railing, he stepped off the porch and headed for his carriage.

"We'll pay it, Mr. Kingman," Ingrid called out to him.

He turned, frowning.

"I am going to marry Carl Unger," she told him. "With what Carl has saved, and by combining this year's profits with his, we'll be able to buy at least one of the farms. The rich man will profit again!" She couldn't hold back her tears. She rose and turned to go inside.

"Ingrid," he shouted.

Ingrid was surprised at his use of her first name, and in such a familiar tone. She faced him again.

"As I said, life just sometimes hands us things we wish it wouldn't," he told her. "I don't know anything about prayer, Miss Svensson, but if you're a praying woman, maybe you should pray about this to that heavenly Father you talked about." He walked closer again, coming up the steps. "And good man or not, Carl Unger isn't right for you. You're too lovely and gentle for him. The fact is, I can't think of any man who's fit for the likes of you."

"I—how would you know such a thing?" she asked, a challenge in her voice.

The look he gave her made her heart pound. "I just know, that's all. I wouldn't rush into anything."

Ingrid stepped back, surprised he would comment on something so personal.

"Combining your farms isn't the answer," he told her. "You probably still won't have enough money, and you'll end up stuck with a man who's all wrong for you." He turned and walked back down the steps. "And, Miss Svensson, if you're going to pray about this," he called out, "say a prayer for me, too." He climbed into his carriage and drove away.

Ingrid watched, confused by some of his remarks about his personal life and his father, remembering how he avoided talking about his mother. She felt a bit stunned over his comments about her and Carl.

Carl Unger isn't right for you.

Why had he said that? What did all of this mean? She put a hand to her heart. Why did he even care whom she married?

She looked down at the paper in her hand. He was probably right about one thing—their combined profits would not be enough money to buy even one of the farms. Tears slipped down her cheeks. "Oh, Far, how can I tell you this news?"

She'd never expected the asking price to be so high. Somehow she'd hoped it wouldn't really come to this, that they would not be among those who received a notice. It was all so unfair. She felt both rage and sorrow. How dare Jude Kingman come here and be such a gentleman and then hand her an eviction notice—and have the audacity to tell her not to marry Carl! The man was out of his mind, or perhaps he simply had an ego the size of a mountain.

Johnny came running up to her then. "Can I eat something, Ingrid?"

Ingrid quickly wiped away her tears. "Come inside. I'll fix you something."

"What did that man want? Did he make you cry?"

Ingrid drew a deep breath. "I'm just tired, Johnny." She turned and went inside to check her bread dough, remembering Kingman's remark about how good it smelled. Men like Jude Kingman had probably never even watched bread being made. He likely only had it served to him on a silver tray, not even caring about the work it took to make it.

Chapter Nine

As Jude gazed at acre after acre of corn that bordered both sides of the dirt road leading to Carl Unger's farm, he thought how unpleasant this visit would be compared to his meeting with Ingrid Svensson two days ago. In spite of his reason for seeing Ingrid, just being around her had made the day enjoyable for him. It would have been a perfect day if he hadn't been compelled to leave her that eviction notice. He suspected he'd made her cry, a fact that had disturbed his sleep, and plagued him with feelings of hatred for his job, his father and himself.

His lack of sleep came from something even

more upsetting than the eviction notice. It was caused primarily by his growing feelings for Ingrid Svensson, feelings that were totally ridiculous and could lead nowhere. If she had any idea she was in his every thought night and day, she'd probably laugh, and so, most certainly, would his own family. They would consider Ingrid totally unfit for the likes of a Kingman, but as far as Jude was concerned, it was the other way around. Ingrid Svensson was too pure, too honest and too unaffected by power and wealth to consider a relationship with a man like himself, a man who represented everything that was wrong in a human being. He shuddered to think how his mother would treat someone like Ingrid and how uncomfortable a down-to-earth woman like Ingrid would feel around his family and associates, or with the "upper crust" of Chicago at one of his mother's parties.

And yet...how she'd shine at something like that, a woman more beautiful without a speck of makeup or a single diamond than all the young women he'd courted in Chicago. He could just imagine how stunning Ingrid would look if she did wear color on her face and had that beautiful blond hair swept up with ruby combs, diamonds gracing her ears and her slender neck, a specially designed ball gown fitted to flatter her figure. People would literally gawk if he walked into the Kingman ball-room with Ingrid Svensson on his arm.

He laughed wryly at his own fantasies.

"Something funny, boss?" Jude's broad-shouldered bodyguard asked. Benjamin was driv-ing the two-seater rig Jude used when bringing an extra man along on some of his visits.

"Just some foolish thinking," he answered.

"Like maybe Carl Unger will greet us with open arms?" Benjamin shouted back, keeping his eyes forward as he snapped the reins. He laughed over his own remark.

"Something like that," Jude lied. He certainly couldn't tell Benjamin he'd been thinking roman-tically about Ingrid Svensson. Besides, Benjamin's remark had spoiled those thoughts and reminded Jude of the reason for today's trip. He actually dreaded even laying eyes on Carl Unger, who not only was one of the more belligerent of the farm-ers on his list, but was also the man who wanted to marry Ingrid.

That's how he thought of her—Ingrid, not Miss Svensson. She had a way of making him feel com-pletely easy around her, as though he'd known her all his life. What fascinated him most was the fact that Ingrid seemed completely unimpressed by his looks, his name or his money. She didn't judge a man by those things, and in that respect Carl Unger probably *was* the better man for her. It was just that he couldn't stomach the thought of someone as lovely and unspoiled as Ingrid being married to someone as crude and uncultured as Carl.

Then again, who was he to judge or advise? Ingrid and Carl had everything in common. They were both children of Swedish immigrants. They both knew and loved farming, both understood and accepted the world in which they lived. Ingrid was most likely perfectly happy with things as they were.

"There's the farm up ahead," Benjamin told him.

Jude straightened, seeing a large wooden barn, well-kept fences and a few cattle and horses about. Everything looked in fine shape, but it irked him that Carl seemed to think more of his barn than his own house. The soddy he lived in was not as neat and tidy as Ingrid's. He thought how, if one really had to live in a dirt house, at least Ingrid's was solid and whitewashed and had wood floors. He suspected this one didn't.

Did Carl Unger expect a woman like Ingrid to live here? Jude's only hope of accepting the idea of Ingrid marrying Unger was if they lived at her farm and not here; or if they lost both farms and

Unger had to find work in town. Maybe at least that way Ingrid could live in a real house, humble as it would likely be.

Still, anyone but Carl would help him rest easier. At least if Ingrid was marrying a man who knew something about culture and refinement, a man who had manners and kept himself clean, a man who had a decent job and would provide a nice home for her, then Jude could bear the thought of her being someone else's bride.

Benjamin drove the carriage closer to the soddy, and Jude noticed an older man out by a pigpen. That would be Carl's father, Stanley. The man exited the pigpen with a large bucket, probably having just fed the snorting, squealing livestock.

"Visitors!" Stanley shouted.

Jude climbed out of the buggy. "Be ready," he told Benjamin.

The front door to the soddy stood open, and in the next moment Carl Unger's huge frame filled the doorway. He held a shotgun in his left hand. "You get off my farm!" he told Jude.

Jude glanced at Benjamin. "Keep your gun holstered." No matter how he felt about Carl Unger, he didn't want to answer to Ingrid if something happened to the man, not to mention that he'd lose any little bit of trust and respect the woman might have for him. "Mr. Unger," he spoke up, "I assure you, I'm not here to destroy everything you and your father have worked for. I'm here to talk about compromises."

"Get off my farm or I vill shoot you!" Carl ordered, raising the shotgun. "I vill not listen to your fancy talk! And I already know you spoke to my Ingrid when she vas alone on her farm. You had no right doing that. You stay away from my Ingrid! It is not proper for a strange man to visit vit a voman alone."

Jude wished he could stop picturing this brute of a man with Ingrid on their wedding night. The thought was enough for him to want to order Benjamin to go ahead and shoot Unger down just to get him out of Ingrid's life.

"Mr. Unger, Miss Svensson was not alone. Her brother was there. And I had no idea her father was gone. Either way, I only went there to serve her an eviction notice."

"And you are here to do the same to *me*! I vill not accept your illegal piece of paper."

"A shotgun and your yelling won't change anything, Mr. Unger. I've not come here to threaten you in the way that you are threatening me right now, and I might remind you I could have my man shoot you for pointing that shotgun at me, but I won't. I'm not out here to draw blood and stir up hatred. I'm just doing my job." He reached into the pocket at the side of his suit jacket and retrieved the notice, then held it out. "This gives you until November, plenty of time to—"

Carl lowered the shotgun barrel slightly and fired, exploding dirt in front of Jude and sending it spraying in a hundred directions, including all over Jude's pants and shoes. Benjamin jumped down from the buggy seat, his handgun drawn.

"You all right, Mr. Kingman?"

"Yes. Put that gun away, Benjamin."

"But, Mr. Kingman—"

"Put it away!" Jude glared at Carl as he spoke, refusing to move one inch. He threw the notice on the ground. "If you want to risk going to prison over this, Mr. Unger, that's your decision, but I might remind you that would mean not being able to marry Miss Svensson, which makes me consider letting you kill me after all. Losing my life might be worth keeping Miss Svensson from becoming your wife. So I suggest that if you truly care about the woman, you set that shotgun aside and let me leave without someone being able to see daylight through my back. Is that possible?"

Carl stared a moment longer, then sighed and lowered the shotgun. "Just this von time. I cannot say that if you come here again I vill not shoot you. Go!"

By then Stanley Unger was standing close. "You go now," he said in a quieter voice. "My son, sometimes he does things vitout thinking."

Does that include someday laying a rough hand on Ingrid because he's angry with her? Jude couldn't help wondering. He turned to Benjamin. "Let's go."

"Kingman!" Carl shouted.

Jude turned.

"What did you mean about keeping Ingrid from marrying me? What right do you have to interfere?"

Jude considered what a fool he was to be so concerned about Ingrid. "No right, Mr. Unger," he answered resignedly. "No right."

"Ya. You remember that. My Ingrid vould never care about a selfish, lying man of vealth who destroys the lives of innocent, hardvorking people. Don't you be thinking about Ingrid Svensson. Men like you, they just use a voman and then throw her avay. You get off my farm and out of my personal business!"

Jude nodded. "You have your notice, Mr. Unger. I'll get off your farm." *But maybe not out of your personal business.* As he climbed into the buggy, Benjamin settled into the driver's seat, never taking his eye off Carl. He picked up the reins and whipped the horse into motion.

"Ya! You go!" Carl yelled after them. "Don't you never come back."

Jude's hands curled into fists. He couldn't care less about what happened here today. He'd expected it. It was the thought of Ingrid being Carl Unger's wife that made his blood boil.

Chapter Ten

Mid-July

Ingrid's head ached from her decision, yet it was best for everyone she cared about, she thought, as she sang along with others in Plum Creek Church, "What a Friend We Have in Jesus."

"Oh, what peace we often forfeit,
Oh, what needless pain we bear.
All because we do not carry
Everything to God in prayer."

She had to hope her own faith and prayer would get her through this. She had agreed to marry Carl. He would always provide for her and Johnny if something should happen to her ailing father, and he would most certainly be a loyal husband. They still clung to the hope that marriage might also save one of the farms. Maybe her father was right when he told her once that a woman could learn to love a man, just for his goodness, and especially after bearing his children.

If only her mother were still alive, she'd have someone to talk to about this. Her doubts and fears were too personal to share with any other woman. Aside from dreading her wedding night, her worry over Carl's anger and aggressiveness was growing. She hoped marrying him would calm him down.

Two weeks ago Carl had stormed to her farm to let her know that he'd done a good job of chasing Mr. Jude Kingman off his land—that he'd shot at the man, not directly, but close enough to show him he meant business. At first Ingrid had felt rage over what Carl had done, and fear for Jude Kingman. The man was so easy to hate, yet she could not help thinking how terrible it would have been if Carl had killed him.

The situation had caused a heated argument between her and Carl, which was followed by apologies and forgiveness, and a promise from Carl that he would never again aim a gun at another man. Ingrid had bribed him into it by promising to set a date for marriage. She thought about Jude's warning that Carl was not the right man for her. Why on earth was a near stranger, especially a man like Jude Kingman, so adamant about whom she should or should not marry? According to Carl, the man had even gone so far as to tell Carl to go ahead and shoot him if he wished, because that way Carl would go to prison and not be able to marry her. What a strange remark for a man of such wealth and power to make about a simple farm girl. If she didn't know better, she'd wonder if Kingman was interested in her romantically.

She shook off the ridiculous thought as the hymn ended and they all took their seats. Ingrid sat between Carl and Johnny, with her father, looking a little more spry today, on the other side of Johnny. Carl's father sat on the other side of Carl, and Ingrid thought what a fine bunch of men they all were.

Yes, this was good. This was perfect. She looked at Carl, and he smiled, then turned his attention to Preacher William Byers who was sermonizing about forbearance when faced with strife, about loving the unlovable and turning the other cheek when an enemy strikes. She could feel

Carl growing a little restless, aware that the preacher was referring to the problems with the railroad.

Suddenly a man in one of the back rows yelled out to the preacher, "I'll not turn *my* other cheek!"

Startled, people turned to look, mumbling among themselves. The man who'd interrupted the sermon was a German farmer, Gunter Sternaman, who'd lived next to Vernon Krueger, the farmer who'd already sold out and moved away.

"Krueger ran off to Omaha with his tail between his legs, but *I* won't!"

Carl rose, putting a fist in the air. "Nor I!" he shouted in reply.

"Carl! We are in God's house!" Ingrid reminded him, trying to keep her voice down.

Carl's father rose. "I do not believe the Good Lord meant for us to turn the other cheek when it means evil winning out over good."

Evil! Were they calling Jude Kingman evil? He most certainly was not, Ingrid thought, wondering why she felt an urge to defend the very man who was evicting her from her own farm. Other men joined in the uproar. Ingrid looked to her father in desperation, glad he at least remained seated.

"I cannot stop them," Albert told her amid the

uproar. Even a few women were railing about the injustice of what was happening.

The entire congregation came alive with comments and arguments over what to do about the railroad. Someone shouted they would never be a traitor to their friends as Vernon Krueger had been. Ingrid felt embarrassed and angry over Carl participating in a shouting match in God's house.

"Please, everyone! This is not the place for this!" Preacher Byers yelled, trying to be heard above the loud anger of the parishioners. "We need to pray about this, not argue."

A few women gathered their children and hurried out of the church, not wanting them to witness all the rage and shouting. Ingrid grasped Carl's arm, forcing him to stop yelling and pay attention to her. "I will not marry a man who behaves like this in the house of God! I thought we settled the issue of your temper, Carl."

She pushed past him and hurried out, wanting to cry. It had been hard enough to make her decision. That, combined with the fear of how on earth they would survive if they lost both farms was wearing on her nerves.

"Ingrid!" She heard Carl call out to her. She turned to see him in the doorway of the small white church they had both attended for years. She waited as he hurried down the steps and strode out to meet her. "I am sorry. I vill try harder to control my temper."

"I don't think you can, Carl! You have changed so much since this thing with the railroad started. Or perhaps you have always been this way and I did not see it! I still cannot believe you actually shot at Jude Kingman!"

"I vould never lose my temper vit you, I swear before God! I just—I vant to give you a good life and to be able to provide for you and our children. I vorry that if I lose the farm, I will not be able to support us, and that upsets me. It comes out in my anger."

Ingrid could see sincerity in his blue eyes. She thought about how he'd been so patient with her about her doubts and indecisions. She grasped his arms.

"Carl, it seems as though this railroad matter has changed all of us. We can't let that happen."

Carl nodded. "I am sorry, Ingrid, but this is all hard on my pride. I vant you to be happy. I vill try very hard to hold my temper, and I vill leave the Grangers if that is what it takes to marry you. Just please set a date that ve vill marry. I love you, Ingrid. When you marry me I vill be the proudest man in Plum Creek—no, in all of Nebraska!"

"Then just tell me you will stop all talk of violence, Carl. We can marry after the harvest. We won't be so busy then, and the railroad matter will be over, one way or another. We might have to give up some things to survive, but we *will* survive. All I want is for all this turmoil and anger to come to an end. I want you out of the Grangers. I want all of this to be over." She led him back up the church steps. "Please go inside and apologize, Carl, right now, to Preacher Myers. And make sure Gunter apologizes, also. See what you can do to calm them all down, and let Preacher Myers pray over this. Please do that for me."

Carl nodded. "Vill you come?"

"In a moment. This is something you should do on your own. I'll go talk to the women sitting at the picnic table over there and see if I can soothe their jangled nerves."

"Ya. Good idea." Carl went inside, and Ingrid turned to go back down the steps. She froze in place when she saw none other than Jude Kingman standing at the bottom of the steps. Her heart raced unexpectedly, and for reasons she could not even understand. She glanced back toward the church entrance before hurrying the rest of the way down the steps.

"Mr. Kingman, this is not a time to be seen

around here!" she warned. "If you were thinking of greeting some of those men when they come out of church, don't do it! They are very angry. An argument broke out in the middle of church services this morning. See what you have done? Men shouting and arguing in God's house!"

Jude looked her over in the strange way he had that brought out feelings no other man, including Carl, had ever stirred in her. "I was standing outside the windows, hoping to get an idea of which way the wind was blowing," he told her. "I got quite an earful."

"Then you already know you had better get out of here, considering that Carl shot at you not long ago." She sighed. "I am very sorry about that. I gave Carl a good scolding for it!"

He chuckled. "I bet you did." He took her arm and pulled her away from the front steps.

Ingrid glanced at the women waiting outside and did not miss their looks of shock and disapproval that she, a single woman and fellow farmer, was talking alone with the enemy.

"It's nice to know you care about my welfare," Kingman told her. He folded his arms authoritatively then, giving her a rather stern gaze. "Sounds like you've decided to marry Mr. Unger after all, from what I just heard the two of you talking about."

"Yes, after the harvest. We will combine our profits and buy one of the farms, or at least enough land to keep farming. You and your railroad men can have the rest of it. I hope that makes you happy, Mr. Kingman."

"I'd be happier to know you weren't marrying Carl Unger." He studied her intently. "You know, not many women have flawless skin even in bright sunlight. But you do. I've never seen anything like it."

Ingrid breathed a sigh of indignation. "Don't change the subject. And as I said, you had better leave."

"But I have some ideas some of those men might like to hear."

"Well, today it's a very *bad* idea even to think about facing those men! And I would suggest, sir, that if you are going to church, your reason might better be to pray for your own soul than to face those men. Besides, a church is considered God's house, and God doesn't need you going in there and creating a ruckus, which I assure you is what would happen. You'd be lucky to leave there with your life."

He frowned. "You mean those Christian men in there might beat me? Or shoot at me again? What kind of church do you go to, Miss Svensson?"

"Please don't mock me, Mr. Kingman. You

know very well the ire you stir in the hearts of the locals."

He leaned a little closer. "And what do I stir in *your* heart, Ingrid? Why do you care that something might happen to me?"

Ingrid backed away slightly, fully aware they were being stared at. She felt embarrassed at what onlookers might be thinking, and at what Jude Kingman might be thinking—that she cared for him more than she had any right to.

"I don't care for your sake, if that's what you think," she protested. "I just do not want Carl or my own father to get in trouble. We do have a sheriff in Plum Creek, you know. Now go!"

He leaned against the side of the church. "I hope you understand that if I had my druthers, I'd find a way to let you keep your farm, Ingrid. Then maybe you would consider being my friend. Maybe you'd even consider allowing me to come courting."

Ingrid's eyes widened in shock. *"What?"*

He flashed the handsome smile that unnerved her. "Please do give more thought to *not* marrying Carl Unger. I still think it's a bad idea."

"Mr. Kingman, I—"

"Hey! You there! Don't be harassing my voman!" Carl's shouted words interrupted their conversation, and the big Swede came storming down the church steps and around to where Ingrid and Jude stood talking.

"Go! Quickly!" Ingrid warned, stepping farther away. She hadn't expected Carl to return so soon. To her amazement, Kingman just stood there, facing Carl squarely. More men came out of church to see what was going on.

"Vat do you think you are doing, showing your face around here on a sacred Sunday, talking to my beloved?" Carl asked. Men gathered behind him. Some of the women walked cautiously closer, shoving children behind their skirts and whispering among themselves.

Ingrid feared a terrible scene that could leave Jude Kingman, and her own reputation, in bad shape. She turned to Carl. "Only moments ago you promised me you'd control your temper from now on, Carl," she reminded him.

"Ya, that is so, but I cannot do so in this case." He kept his eyes on Jude Kingman as he spoke. "You get out of here! I chased you off my property when you came there vit your illegal papers, and now I order you out of Plum Creek. I missed you with my shotgun on purpose the first time. The next time I vill not miss!"

"Carl!" Ingrid could hardly believe her ears after the promises Carl had just made to her.

"None of us vill move, *ever*," Carl added, "no matter what legal documents you try to force on us!"

The men behind Carl shouted their agreement with Carl's remark.

Kingman just shook his head, moving even closer to Carl. He stood nearly as tall, and his dark eyes narrowed. "Mr. Unger, I told you before, this is something that simply can't be stopped, even if you shoot me and anyone else who comes after me. You'll just get in even more trouble, so why don't you and the others here just decide how you can pool your money and save at least *some* of your farms, and quit this crazy talk? Doing something illegal will just cost all of you money and anguish."

"*Illegal!* You talk to us about doing something illegal?" Carl fumed right back. He raised a fist to hit Kingman, and Ingrid gasped when Kingman blocked the big man's blow with his left hand, then pushed him away with such force that Carl fell sprawling on his back.

Women gasped, and Ingrid's eyes widened in shock, surprised that a burly man like Carl could be felled by a fancy man like Jude Kingman, though he was a well-built man.

No one made a move as Kingman glared at Carl. "That's twice you've threatened me with physical harm," he told the Swede. "I could have hit you instead of just defending myself, and I could legally have had my man shoot you that day you fired at me, Unger, but I *didn't*, did I? *Think about that.*" He turned to Ingrid. "It so happens that I excelled at athletics at Yale," he explained, "and, by the way, my ill feelings toward Carl aren't just because he shot at me," he added, a startlingly intense look in his eyes. "I think you know what I mean." He turned and walked toward the railroad yard, and Ingrid watched after him, dumbstruck.

Carl managed to get to his feet and he pointed as he addressed the others. "Look at the coward, hurrying away! He vill not stay around to finish a fight!"

Carl was obviously embarrassed at being knocked flat by a man he considered a dire enemy. Still, it was Carl who'd started it all. Ingrid looked up at him. "You were going to strike him first, Carl! What happened to everything we just talked about? And what did you mean about not missing the next time you point a gun at Jude Kingman? I've told you how I feel about guns and violence!"

"What I promised you does not apply to that man! You stay avay from him!"

"I was only warning him off!" Ingrid turned and hurried toward the family wagon, her mind and heart spinning with confusion over Jude Kingman's remark about courting her. *Courting* her...it was something she'd daydreamed about, being formally courted by a gentleman, not grabbed and yelled at and ordered around by a brute or choosing to marry just to seal a business deal.

Still, what choice did she have? It was silly to believe that the likes of Jude Kingman would truly be remotely interested in a Nebraska farm girl. The man must be out of his mind...or cleverly trying to win her over just to get his way. And to entertain one romantic thought about Jude Kingman was nothing short of betrayal toward her father and brother and the whole town of Plum Creek!

Chapter Eleven

Late July

Ingrid pulled bread from the oven and set it on the table to cool. She then put in a blackberry pie to bake, thinking what a fine dessert it would make this evening when her father and Johnny returned home from Plum Creek. Although he and Carl had both promised to drop out of the Grangers, they had practically begged her to let them go to one more meeting. Since Ingrid needed more sugar and flour and four more yards of heavy blue cotton cloth to make more pants for a growing

Johnny, she'd allowed her father to go to the meeting as long as he promised to bring home the things she needed. Johnny had pestered her to let him go, too, as a trip to Plum Creek was always a matter of excitement to him.

She was angry with herself for giving in to them all, but her decision had been partially motivated by a selfish desire to have a day alone. She was weary of all the talk of the railroad and the Grangers and lawsuits and evictions and worry over crop yields. But most of all, she wanted a day away from men in general. It was nice to have peace and quiet, nice to have a day to herself and one that was relatively free of chores. She'd finished the weekly wash the day before, and all the animals had been fed, the cows milked, eggs collected, and there wasn't a lot to do for the corn at this point but watch it grow and hope it didn't dry up or disappear due to the appetites of hungry worms.

After Albert and Johnny left this morning she'd bathed and decided to wear one of her better day dresses, a simple blue-checked dress that she never wore when there were heavy chores to do. She'd left her hair long and loose, pulling it up at the sides only. With no one here to see her, she'd decided there was nothing improper about leaving it down.

She began humming a Swedish tune her mother

used to sing, one she'd always remembered. Singing made her feel better. She needed to convince herself life would be just fine, and baking bread and pies and cleaning up the house reminded her she would one day soon be doing these things for Carl. She would have a husband and maybe not long after that a baby to hold and love and take her mind and heart off of this terrible summer's events. Maybe she and Carl would even be living in town, which was not such a bad thing. Maybe they would have a real house, with an upstairs and maybe even a piano, so if she had a daughter she could take lessons. Their daughter could play and sing and fill their house with happiness.

She sat down, staring at her prized possession, her Concord range. Yes, she told herself, this could all work out for the best. She would learn to love Carl and her father would have help.

She sighed. She was happy. Yes, she was happy. She and Carl would have a lovely wedding at the little church in Plum Creek. The railroad matter would be settled one way or another, and because of that, Carl's anger would be gone and he'd be pleasant and accommodating. He'd be a good husband and father.

The tears came then. What was she going to do? She wasn't happy at all, and, no, things were not working out just fine. She'd never felt more lonely in her entire life, and the thought of being Carl's wife threw her into despair. But what else could she do? Marrying Carl was the only option. If it made her terribly unhappy, she would make up for it through making *others* happy, through being a good wife and sister and daughter, and she would find all the love she needed when she had babies. That would mend everything, wouldn't it?

She chastised herself for not being grateful for the good things in her life, her health, her sweet brother, her kind father and Carl, who did truly love her, even though he had no idea how to show love or tenderness. How many women were lucky enough to be marrying such a good, strong, dependable man?

When she heard someone ride up outside, she wiped at her tears and straightened. Who on earth could be here? It upset her to think someone had come visiting on the very day she'd planned to have time alone. And here she was with her hair down! She quickly rose and smoothed her apron, again wiping at her tears and hoping her eyes weren't swollen. She grabbed a handkerchief and blew her nose, taking a deep breath before going to the door.

Her eyes widened and her heart raced when

through the screen she saw none other than Jude Kingman dismounting his beautiful black horse, which he'd ridden himself this time rather than bringing a buggy. He wore dark pants and shiny knee-high boots, a soft blue shirt and a black leather vest, as well as a wide-brimmed hat and black leather gloves. He tied the horse and glanced at the doorway.

"Good. You *are* home alone," he said.

The words made her wary. She latched the hook on the screen door. "What are you doing here, Mr. Kingman?"

He frowned as he stepped up on the wooden stoop. "My goodness, are you locking me out? Don't tell me you're *afraid* of me!"

"Well…no…but I *am* here alone, and it wouldn't be proper to let in you, of all people. And I have not even pinned up my hair."

He rested one hand against the doorjamb, peering at her through the screen. "I can see that. And you have the prettiest hair I've ever seen. You should always wear it down like that."

Ingrid felt a headache coming on. "Please leave, Mr. Kingman."

"Call me Jude. And didn't I tell you I might come courting?"

She felt a flush come into her cheeks. "Don't

make fun, Mr. Kingman. No man of your standing would court a farm girl. I do not appreciate this."

He straightened, sighing. "How many times do I have to tell you people that one thing I don't do is lie? And how do you know what a man like me wants? Maybe I just like talking to you. Goodness knows I don't have a friend between here and Chicago. Can't we at least be that? Friends? And can't I *please* have a piece of that bread I smell? The last time I was here it wasn't finished baking. Are you really going to turn me away again without letting me have some?"

Ingrid just stared at him a moment, wishing she could determine whether or not the man could truly be trusted. "First tell me why you came here knowing I was alone. A young woman's father should be present when a man comes courting, if you insist on calling it that. And how did you even know my father was gone?"

He folded his arms. "Because I know there is a Granger meeting today, and I suspected your beloved Carl would not keep his promise and stay away. I had one of my men keep an eye out, and when I was told Carl and your father and even your brother had gone to the meeting, I mounted my horse and came straight here. I figured riding the horse rather than using a buggy would get me here even faster so I could have a few minutes alone with you and then get out of here before your father returns. I promise that I won't let him catch me here and no one else will ever know I came." He leaned closer again. "And need I tell you how easily I could break through this flimsy screen door if I wanted to?"

Ingrid could not deny that she felt a certain curiosity about whether this man might actually want to be her friend. "Well, for once you have not caught me in filthy work clothes and with kerosene on my hands," she answered, unlatching the door. She stepped back and let him inside. His tall, well-built frame seemed to fill the room, yet in a different way than Carl did. And she had to admit that he smelled wonderful. How did the man do that? She imagined he must use some kind of expensive men's cologne that the average person could never afford.

He removed his hat and bowed slightly. "Thank you, Ingrid. And I am still waiting for you to call me Jude."

She fought disturbing emotions that, though puzzling and indefinable, seemed sinfully wrong. She was engaged to Carl, the only kind of man for whom she was fit, a man who knew and understood her world. A man like Jude Kingman was not only far beyond her grasp, but most likely someone who dangled women on a string for as long as he wanted and then tossed them away when he moved on to another conquest. How many hearts had the man broken?

"I only use first names with people I know extremely well, Mr. Kingman, and I don't know you at all. However, I don't want to be rude. You may sit down at the kitchen table and I will set out some butter and slice you some bread."

He smiled, a smile that seemed so genuine. He sat down at the crude, handmade table, and Ingrid nervously set out the butter and a knife, a couple of small china plates and cups.

"Would you like coffee?"

"Sounds wonderful."

"You cannot stay long, Mr. Kingman. I am truly worried someone will find you here."

"I'll make sure to be gone in plenty of time."

Ingrid set a loaf of bread on a cutting board and carefully sliced it. "It is still hot, which makes it more difficult to cut," she explained.

"Ah, but more delicious to eat," he added.

Ingrid relaxed a little. After cutting several slices she took a porcelain kettle from the stove and poured coffee into two cups, then sat down across the table from him. "I will let you butter your own bread. Everyone does it differently, I've learned."

He picked up the knife. "Me, I like lots of butter. With bread this warm I'll have the butter dripping off. I suppose you also churned this butter yourself."

"I did." Ingrid sipped her coffee while he buttered his bread and took a bite. He rolled his eyes in a gesture of sheer pleasure. "Delicious," he said after swallowing. "How do you do it?"

Ingrid blushed. "I have been kneading and baking bread and helping churn butter since I was five years old. When you live on a farm, Mr. Kingman, you learn at an early age how to do such things. Everyone shares in the chores."

"And that is one of the things I admire about you. You're so self-sufficient. The women I know in Chicago usually have others do everything for them. They are waited on hand and foot and can hardly run a comb through their hair by themselves. It's ridiculous—and boring."

Ingrid studied him a moment as he ate more of the bread. "Are *you* waited on hand and foot, Mr. Kingman?" she asked.

He chuckled. "Sometimes."

"Well, then, you would never be happy with a woman like me. I will not be a servant, Mr. Kingman. Perhaps that is how you picture me."

He drank some coffee, suddenly very serious. "I don't think of you that way at all, Ingrid. I think of you as the most beautiful and unusual and strong woman I've ever met, and I have a great deal of admiration and respect for you. And although I will probably make you very angry, I am asking you again not to marry Carl Unger."

Ingrid closed her eyes in exasperation. "Is *that* why you're here?"

"Not the only reason, but the primary one."

"Mr. Kingman, it is truly none of your business whom I choose to marry."

"It *is* my business, because I think you're marrying Carl Unger strictly to make other people happy and in hopes of saving one of the farms. That would make it my fault that you're married to a brute of a man who can never make you truly happy and who I fear could even become mean and demanding once the bloom of being newlyweds wears off. You are a very special woman who deserves a very special man. I wish I could be that man. Though I would like nothing more than to be to court you, in truth I know we are likely far too different to make anything like that work, but if I can't have you, then I'd at least like to see you with a decent man who will properly care for you, respect you, give you a nice home and never abuse you."

Ingrid shook her head in wonder, angry with him for expressing all her own doubts about Carl, just when she'd decided marrying him was the right thing to do. "I don't understand you, Mr. Kingman." She turned in her chair, refusing to meet his eyes. "Why, oh, why do you care so much? It makes no sense, especially considering that you came here to throw me off my land."

He leaned forward, resting his elbows on the table. "I didn't expect to run into someone like you. I didn't expect to care about you or any of the others around here, but I *do* care, Ingrid. I want you to know that. I want you to believe me when I say I don't like what I'm doing, but it's going to be done, whether by me or someone else. If I hadn't come here, someone much less caring would be here and all of you would already be gone, homeless and jobless. I'm trying to avoid that, but those idiots at that Granger meeting don't understand. So if I can get one bit of comfort out of all of this, it would be to know that although I've taken this farm away, I have at least kept you from making matters worse by throwing your life away on Carl Unger!"

Ingrid struggled not to break into tears again. She swallowed more coffee. "You have said what you came to say, Mr. Kingman. When you finish your bread, you should go." She drew a deep breath, still avoiding his gaze. "And if you are truly sincere in the things you say, then I thank you for your concern. But when all this is over, you will return to Chicago and your busy but comfortable life there and enjoy your wealth and go on to other things, while I am left with an aging, ailing father and a young brother who still has much growing to do. That leaves me as the one to whom both will turn for support." Finally she met his dark eyes. "And no matter how strong you think I am, I cannot do it all alone. A man like Carl will find a way to provide for all of us, even if he must give up his farm. Perhaps, Mr. Kingman, if just once in your life you had to wonder where your next bite of bread would come from, you would understand that sometimes a person has to make sacrifices to survive in this world."

A look of admiration showed in his eyes, catching Ingrid off guard. "Giving things up and working harder than ever are acceptable sacrifices. But offering yourself up like a lamb to the slaughter is quite another. It isn't necessary. And if I have to buy your farm myself and give it back to you to keep you from marrying that man, then I'll do it."

"*Nej!*" She shook her head. "I would never accept a handout from you!" she answered. "Nor would my father. Surely you know that. Do not even suggest such a thing. We will make do, Mr. Kingman. You have done your job, and I understand this is railroad business and not truly your personal choice. You can rest assured that I do not blame you for all of this. But neither will I allow or accept special favors from you when so many others will also suffer."

"Fine. But what about Carl? Are you still going to marry him?"

Now her head truly did ache. "I will...I will give more thought to it and...I will look into other options, if that will ease your conscience, Mr. Kingman."

"I don't care about my conscience. I care about you, more than you realize. In fact, the only reason I won't pursue my feelings any further is because I'm intelligent enough to realize you wouldn't be any more happy in my world than you would being married to Carl. You'd hate living like a Kingman, and you'd have no use for the kind of people we mix with, and they in turn would be cruel and disrespectful toward you. And it might surprise you to know that in spite of my Yale education, my wealth and the power of the Kingman name, I am a very unhappy man. Meeting you hasn't helped any, because now I want something I can't have, and believe me, that is not a situation to which I am accustomed."

Ingrid was unable to suppress a smile. "I am sure it isn't." She couldn't help thinking what a wonderful life she might have with a man like Jude Kingman, if only he didn't come with the baggage of his name and power. "I am sorry you are not happy, Mr. Kingman. I do not understand all the reasons, but I will pray for you. I fear your feelings for me stem only from the fact that you are unhappy, and that you are simply looking for something different in your life because you think it will change it for the better. If I was certain that was not the case, I would take more seriously your kind words and your offer of friendship. But we both know that it could never work. Surely among the wealthier, more educated young women in Chicago there is one who is not pampered and spoiled and weak. Seek and ye shall find, Mr. Kingman. God loves you just as much as He loves me or anyone else, and if you pray to Him, He will help you find whatever it is you are looking for."

Again the look in his eyes stirred feelings that were new to her.

"Then I guess I have to pray that somehow your God leads me right back to you," he told her. He downed the rest of his coffee. "Thank you for the good coffee and wonderful bread," he said, rising.

Ingrid also stood. Something about him made her want to reach out to him, but she kept her distance. "Perhaps you should take the rest of the loaf, Mr. Kingman. I would have trouble explaining to Far how I managed to eat so much of it myself. If the entire loaf is gone, he will never know I baked more than two loaves."

"Good idea. I'd love to take it with me."

Ingrid walked to a cupboard and took out some brown wrapping paper she always saved from shopping. She set the bread in it and wrapped it, then tied string around it. All the while she felt Jude's eyes on her, and she couldn't help wondering what it might be like to have such a man love her. She handed out the loaf of bread, and he grasped one of her hands as he took it.

"Tell me you won't marry Carl," he asked again. "If I start praying about this, then we need to give God time to show us His answer, don't we? He can't do that if you marry Carl before we know what is really supposed to happen in our lives."

His touch made her tremble, and she could no longer fight her deeper conviction that she would never be happy with Carl. It had nothing to do with what Jude was asking of her. It was simply fact.

She pulled her hand away and nodded. "I will not marry Carl," she answered. "I am not saying never. I am only saying I'll not marry him right now, and not just to save a farm." She met his eyes. "And it has nothing to do with you, Mr. Kingman. It simply has to do with what is right."

Jude nodded. "I understand." He suddenly frowned. "Is that some kind of pie I smell baking?"

Grateful for the change of subject, Ingrid smiled. "Yes, a berry pie. And no, you cannot take it with you. It is not finished, and besides that, I promised my father and brother that they would be eating berry pie tonight for dessert."

Jude chuckled. "Never hurts to ask." He glanced at her Concord. "That's quite a cooking range you have there."

"It is my pride and joy. I regret that I may have to sell it when we lose the farm. We will have to sell a lot of things, Mr. Kingman, in order to have the money to settle somewhere else, and until we find work."

He smiled sadly. "In my world it's her diamonds and furs a woman would miss if she lost everything," he told her. "How refreshing to meet someone who would miss something as simple as a cooking range."

He turned and walked out. Ingrid went to the

door to watch him mount up. He looked quite grand on the black gelding. She supposed his family had a huge stable of fine horses and carriages back in Chicago.

Holding the loaf of bread in one hand, he took the reins in his other hand and nodded to her. "Thank you—for everything," he told her. "I'll go around the corn fields and take a different way back to Plum Creek, in case your father is headed home along the main road."

She nodded. "Thank you. God be with you, Mr. Kingman."

"As I am sure He is already with you," he replied. He turned the horse and rode off. Ingrid watched him for as long as she could. By the end of summer he would be out of her life, and it struck her that she would feel very sad about that.

Chapter Twelve

Early August

"Well, now, where is Wilson?" Jude studied his brother suspiciously as he walked into Wilson Beyer's office in Omaha to find Mark sitting behind the man's desk.

"I gave him the day off."

Jude hung his hat on a hat tree, then removed his suit jacket because of the warm weather. "Decided you wanted to enjoy the weather down here in dusty farm country, did you?"

"You know how I love farmers and dirt and cattle and all that."

"I know enough that you aren't here for a pleasant vacation." Jude sighed in exasperation, folding his arms and facing Mark. "What gives you the right to come into my territory and give my employee the day off? I needed to talk to Wilson."

"You can talk to me, brother."

Jude caught an all-too-familiar arrogance in the remark. "No, I can't—and I won't. If Wilson isn't here, then that cancels the whole reason I'm here. You and I have nothing to talk about."

Mark leaned forward, grinning slyly. "Not necessarily—if it's about the settlers you were supposed to get off railroad land. Last time I talked to Wilson, he said you hadn't accomplished much."

"Is that so?" Jude eyed the man narrowly as he took a chair across from the desk. "Well, that's none of your business. I was given this job to handle as I see fit."

"Anything that displeases Father *is* my business. He's not going to be very happy with your lack of progress, big brother."

"Well, why don't you let me worry about that? You certainly have no trouble pleasing him."

Deep satisfaction and a spark of triumph came

into Mark's eyes. "I don't, do I? Have you ever wondered why that is?"

Jude leaned back, putting his feet up on the desk. "Actually, I have. Many times. But for the moment my only concern is why you are here. I'm taking care of things just fine. I've given all the settlers their walking papers. They have until November first to come up with the necessary money or get out. A few have already left, and one even took a job I found for him here in Omaha. So far I've managed to approach this thing in a way that has kept things fairly peaceful."

"And do you really think Dad or I care about settling this peacefully? We just want it settled— period."

"We? What's this? Are you in a partnership with our father, the two of you against me?"

Mark sighed and leaned back. "I just know how Dad thinks, that's all. And I know how *you* think. A good businessman can't also be a peacemaker, Jude. And he doesn't give his enemies chances."

"These people aren't enemies. They are just human beings who love their land and aren't going to up and leave it willingly or without trying to find a way to keep it."

"That's the whole point. You don't give them the opportunity to keep it. You have to do something to take away whatever hope these people might have, dishearten them somehow, maybe even scare them out."

"You can just forget that kind of talk. Dad gave me this job, Mark. I'll take care of it the way I see fit. Why don't you go back to Chicago and take care of the things you're *supposed* to be taking care of?"

"I'm sure you'd like that. But I told Dad I'd come down here and see how things were going. Wilson says one of the bigger troublemakers and more stubborn of the settlers is some big Swede named Carl Unger, him and a man named Gunter Sternaman. That so?"

Jude shrugged. "Among others."

"And need I remind you there are ways of taking care of people like that?"

"Like going in there with a gang of henchmen and tossing them off their land?"

"If necessary."

"We live in a democracy, remember? We have no right using force in a matter that the courts can deal with. All we can do is try to convince most of them they can't afford a legal battle and would be wise to get out now with this year's profits. If we offer them other jobs, we give them some hope and they are more willing to leave."

"I see." Mark raised his eyebrows and grinned an almost evil grin. "I might remind you, Jude, that Dad sent you down here to get rid of those farmers, not give them time to think, not present other options, not give them the opportunity to make a profit this year. Some of them could use that money to buy their farms. We don't want that, and you aren't supposed to let that happen. Get them out of there *before* harvest. For crying out loud, Jude, do your job and get this over with so we can go forward and start making real money off of that land."

Jude glared at him, wondering if their father really did know Mark was here. "I don't answer to you, Mark, and if I ever had to, I'd quit Kingman Enterprises and go off on my own. I'll tell you again, this is my job to handle as I see fit, so get out of that chair and go home. Practice your bossy arrogance on those who take you seriously, and who are intimidated by you, because I'm not. And if Dad seriously disagreed with what I'm doing, *he'd* be sitting in that chair right now, not you." He watched the blood rise to his brother's face.

"Be that as it may, Jude, you want to impress Dad with this job and everything else you do for him. I know you. You'll do anything to win Dad's approval—and affection—which brings me to a subject regarding another area in which you may disappoint Dad, and most certainly Mother."

Jude leaned forward, fuming inside. "Of course I want Dad's approval, but unlike you, Mark, I am my own man, and if what Dad wants goes against what is right, then I'll choose my own path. Right now I couldn't care less about anything else you think might gain Dad's disapproval." He rose from his chair, fed up with their conversation.

"Not even if that little matter about Dad's disapproval involves a young woman by the name of Ingrid Svensson?"

Jude froze, his rage suddenly growing.

"I see I've hit a nerve, brother. I had a little talk with your man Benjamin when you let him come back to Chicago for a few days to see his wife and kids. He told me about some beautiful Swedish woman who is set to be kicked off her land and who he believes caught your eye. Now, I know your reputation with women. I do hope she's nothing but another romp in the hay for you."

Mark's eyes bulged with fear when Jude whipped around, slapped his hands on the desk, and leaned forward so that his face was just a few inches from Mark's. "If you ever again insinuate that Ingrid Svensson is anything but respectable," he said in a dangerously low tone, "I'll make sure you regret it, even if it costs me my whole inheritance, you selfish, worthless ingrate!" Jude shoved away from the desk so hard that it slid forward to press against his brother's waist. "Now, get out of here!" he raged.

Mark cussed as he pushed the desk away and stood. He straightened his clothes and ran a hand through his hair. "Well, well, well." He pretended to be unaffected. "Seems you're actually sweet on some dirt-poor foreign milkmaid." He sniffed, raising his chin. "That would be just like you. You could have any woman you want with your looks, all of them already rich and beautiful. But no, you're attracted to some Swedish farm girl." He walked around the other side of the desk, well away from Jude. He took his hat from the coat tree. "Well, *big* brother, I hope you aren't thinking of bringing such a woman into the family. She'd never be welcome, you know, and would never fit in. Don't go and do something stupid, Jude. You're in enough trouble at the moment."

"If I never bring Ingrid Svensson to Chicago, it will be because I'd be too embarrassed for her to meet the likes of you! She's a far better person than you *or* I can ever hope to be!"

His brother cautiously made his way to the door. "Get rid of those farmers, Jude, especially the rebellious ones like Carl Unger. For crying out loud the man shot at you! There is only one way to deal with men like that."

Jude stepped closer then, towering over his much shorter brother. "Like what?"

Mark opened the door as though to make a quick getaway. "You know what I mean, and *I'm* the man for it." He stepped into the hallway, addressing Jude through the open doorway. "And if you bring home that ignorant farm woman who likely has the grace of a cow, mother will shriek so loud they'll hear it all over Chicago."

"I couldn't care less what Corrine thinks of anything," Jude sneered. "And it would be nice if you wouldn't go running to her like a runny-nosed kid every time you don't get something you want. Grow up!"

Mark looked him over. "Don't underestimate what I might do to prove to Dad that I'm the better man for this job." The old rivalrous jealousy showed in his hard eyes. "But I'll give you a little more time. For now you can have the dust and the corn and the cow manure all to yourself, along with your little Swedish dish."

Mark hurried away and Jude slammed the door behind them, more upset over Mark's remark about Ingrid than his interference in things that didn't concern him. He couldn't bear to hear any man, especially one as worthless as Mark, insult Ingrid.

He turned and swept his arm over the desk, knocking everything off it, realizing his powerfully emotional reaction to Mark's words only verified his own awakening truth—and fear. He was indeed in love with Ingrid Svensson, a woman who could never be a part of his world, and of whom he was totally unworthy. The one thing he had—money—meant nothing to her. The things that meant most to her were character and faith— and he had neither.

Chapter Thirteen

Mid-August

"Are you sure, Ingrid? What about your idea to combine our profits and save at least von of the farms? People in town expect you to marry Carl. Ve have already told them you vill, let alone that you have told Carl."

Ingrid finished tying her slat bonnet as she stood in the kitchen. "I wanted very much to marry Carl, Far. It was the practical thing to do, but I just cannot go through with it. I simply do not love him."

"You vill *learn* to love him."

Ingrid faced her pleading father. "You keep saying so, Far, but do you truly believe that? Is that what Mama had to do? *Learn* to love you?"

"Vell, no. I mean, ve vere in love, but—"

"Would you expect less for me? Do you really want your daughter to marry a man she does not love?"

"But I thought you *did* love Carl. You already told him you vould marry him."

She lowered her head. "For the wrong reasons, Far, and I am sorry about that. I was trying to convince myself that I could do this, but I just can't. I know you fear I will never marry, but I *will*, when the time is right, when God sends the right man. I just do not believe Carl is that man. I know it is unfair to change my mind, but it would be cruel and unfair to Carl to pretend that I love him. He deserves better than that."

Albert sighed and shook his head. "You vill break his heart."

"There are other young girls in Plum Creek who would love to marry such a solid, dependable man. Carl will be fine."

Albert stepped closer. "Vat are you not telling me, daughter? Vat has *really* changed your mind?"

Ingrid frowned, refusing to face a truth she feared her father suspected. "I don't know what you mean."

"You *do* know. All of this strange behavior started after our first visit from that railroad man."

Ingrid looked away. "Mr. Kingman has nothing to do with it."

"Doesn't he?"

"Of course not!" Ingrid whirled. "He came here to steal our farm, for goodness' sake! And he comes from a world I have never seen and do not desire. But you should know that the few times I have talked to him he showed nothing but respect and a desire to make things as easy for us as possible. He is a better man than you think, Far, but he has nothing to do with my decision about Carl. I have never loved Carl in the way a woman should love the man she marries. It's that simple."

Albert shook his head. "Then I am glad my back is better. If you do not marry Carl then that means I cannot expect as much help from him. He vill have his own future to vorry about." He walked to gaze through the screen door. "It might not matter after all. Look out there. No rain for almost six veeks. The corn should already be three to four feet high, and it is barely two." He shook his head. "Ve vill lose this place, Ingrid. The railroad can afford the best lawyers, and the Grangers are not moving fast enough to stop all of this." He looked at her sadly. "I thought ve had so much opportunity when ve first came to America. I vas so happy when I got this land and thought it vas free only for farming it. Your beloved mother died helping me farm this land. Now the railroad vill sell it for a lot of money—" anger came into his eyes "—*blood* money! *Our* blood!"

Ingrid reached out and cautiously put a hand on his shoulder. "God will take care of us, Far. I am young and so is Johnny. We can both work in town if we must. We will survive. You have worked hard all these years to provide for us. Now we will find a way to provide for you and keep us all together. I am not afraid."

He turned away. "It is not right. It just is not right."

"We have had many good years here, Far. And we even have a little money saved. We have plenty of tools and equipment to sell, along with the plow horses, the cattle, pigs, chickens. With what we will make this year on our crops, we should have enough to rent a house in town. Or maybe Mr. Kingman will allow us to buy the land by making payments."

"At railroad interest rates?" He glanced at her with a look of disgust. "Eighteen percent!" He waved her off. "Go now. Go and break Carl's heart."

Ingrid sighed with frustration. Her decision had

caused a rift with her father, and now she worried how Carl would react. "I truly am sorry, Far."

She walked out and climbed into the wagon, which Johnny had hitched for her to one of the big, gray plow horses. She slapped the reins and got the horse underway, setting out on the two-mile trek to Carl's house. She felt her whole life being turned upside down, and she would soon turn Carl's upside down, also.

Was her father right? *Did* this have something to do with Jude Kingman? No, it was impossible. She simply did not love Carl Unger. She cared for him as a dear friend, but it could never be anything more.

All the way to Carl's farm she practiced what she would tell him, how she would tell him. She prayed he would not be too angry. Finally, after nearly a half hour of bouncing over the narrow dirt road, Carl's farm came into sight. It was so well kept, the buildings sturdy. She'd been in the Unger soddy before, plain and not as well kept. It sorely needed a woman's touch in decorating. That would have to wait for the right woman.

She steered the horse along the drive, thinking how Carl's corn seemed a little higher than their own. Carl was a fine farmer—had a way of making something out of nothing. Her heart beat faster as she came closer and she again went over in her mind how she would tell Carl that she could not marry him after all.

As the wagon approached the soddy, she saw something odd on the steps to the front porch of Carl's house. It looked like—

"No!"

A body lay sprawled on the wooden steps.

"No!"

She snapped the reins, and the horse drew the buggy to within a few feet of the front steps. Ingrid jerked the reins to stop the animal, then quickly slammed a foot against the wagon brake and sat staring for a moment. What she saw surely wasn't real!

"Carl?" she called out, hoping maybe he'd fallen and she could find a way to help him. "Carl?"

She looked around. Was someone here? She saw nothing unusual. She gathered her wits and climbed down from the wagon, her heart pounding with trepidation. The way Carl lay sprawled on the steps just seemed odd. When she drew closer, she gasped, "No!"

Blood stained the front of his shirt. She looked around again. "Stanley!" she yelled for Carl's father. There came no answer; everything seemed extraordinarily quiet. As she scanned the surroundings, she saw chickens strutting around, pecking at whatever they could find to eat. Then she saw two of Carl's three plow horses lying on their sides near the barn. They were totally still, and gut instinct told her they were dead.

She looked back at Carl, and it took a great deal of effort to make her legs move so she could walk closer to him. She grasped her roiling stomach—he'd been shot! She didn't need to touch him to realize that he, too, was dead. She couldn't find her voice, and she didn't know if she should run, although she wanted to. Struggling against a horrible lump in her throat and trying not to panic, she walked carefully around Carl. The front door to his small soddy stood open.

What if the killers were still inside? And who on earth would do this? Indians? There had been no trouble with them around here for years. And they would not have left the bodies intact, nor would they kill horses.

Robbers? Carl and Stanley had nothing of value to steal. What money they'd saved was in a bank in Plum Creek. And why would someone shoot good, strong plow horses rather than steal them?

She managed to catch her breath, and as her eyes began to fill with tears, she cautiously went inside the house. There, on the floor, lay Stanley, shot in the back.

"Oh, no! No!" Finally she found her voice, and it came out in a scream. "Nooooo!" She had to get her father. And he should get some other men together before coming back here. She ran back outside, looking once more at poor Carl. Guilt flooded her being. She should have married the poor man a long time ago and brought him some little bit of happiness. Now she felt bad for not being able to love him. Still, if she'd been here, too—and if her father and Johnny had also been living here—they could all be dead!

She ran to the wagon, her breath coming in deep sobs now, her mind whirling with the possibilities of what could have happened here.

Hardly able to see from crying, she managed to pick up the reins and kick off the wagon brake. She slapped the horse's rump and sent the gelding into a full run toward home.

One other possibility began to creep into her mind, a possibility she could hardly bear to acknowledge. When a crime was committed, one had to think first about who would benefit. In Carl's case, only one entity would benefit from his and his father's deaths: the railroad. That meant...Jude Kingman.

Chapter Fourteen

Ingrid stared at the open graves beneath the rope slings that held Carl's and Stanley's plain wooden caskets. Neighbors had brought the bodies to Plum Creek for the wake and for burial in the town cemetery.

Ingrid could still hardly believe that a big, solid, good-hearted man like Carl was gone. She kept expecting him to show up at the farm for a visit, or even to walk up behind her now and ask why she was so upset.

"'But Christ has indeed been raised from the dead,'" Preacher Byers read from 1 Corinthians, "'the first fruits of those who have fallen asleep. For since death came through a man, the resurrection of the dead comes also through a man. For as in Adam all die, so in Christ all will be made alive.'"

Ingrid hardly heard the preacher's words. So much in her life had changed since that first visit from Jude Kingman. Carl's disposition had changed; the good feelings among everyone in town had changed; hope for the future had vanished. The excitement of planting had given way to the worry of losing most of the crop because of drought. And it looked more and more as though it would be impossible to save their own farm, land that should have gone one day to Johnny.

If for some reason God had decided to test her faith, He was certainly doing a good job of it. And now many in town seemed to be forgetting their Christian morals altogether. Men and women were up in arms, all of them sure the railroad was to blame for the deaths of the Ungers. Many were naming Jude Kingman in particular, saying he must have ordered the murders.

Ingrid did not want to believe that, but what did she really know about the man? And deep inside she couldn't help wondering if Kingman might have had a double purpose. He hadn't wanted her to marry Carl. Surely that hadn't been so important to him that he'd kill the poor man! She simply could not imagine such a thing. Still, just how far would someone as powerful as Jude go to get what he wanted?

Another part of her prayed none of those thoughts could possibly be true. She actually feared for Jude's life if and when he came back from another trip to Omaha. But she shouldn't even care. It was his fault she'd felt torn in every direction the past several weeks, confused, depressed and worried about the railroad taking the farm, in a turmoil over her feelings for Carl.

And now this: the terrible guilt of having repeatedly turned down the marriage proposal of a man who was soon to be murdered. At least she'd finally accepted and he'd died still thinking she would marry him.

She wept as the casket was lowered after the final prayer. Everyone sang,

"How happy every child of grace,
Who knows his sins forgiven!
This earth, he cries, is not my place
I seek my place in heaven."

Ingrid's throat was too sore and choked to join in. Poor, sweet Carl. Had he suffered? Who could do such a thing? It appeared to have been an execution. Nothing had been stolen or ransacked. There simply appeared to be no earthly reason for the deaths.

The funeral ended, and the grumbling began.

"This is nothing more than a message from the railroad!" one man fumed as the crowd began to break up. "They want us to be afraid to stand against them!"

"Sure, but try to prove it!" another answered. "No one heard anything, saw anything, or even heard death threats. And the railroad didn't need to kill anyone to get what they wanted. All they needed was to use the law to run us out."

"I say we lynch that Jude Kingman the next time he shows his face," the first man declared.

"Stop it, all of you!" Ingrid found herself speaking up. "No Christian, man or woman, should speak of such things! I agree with Mr. Connelley that the railroad would not need to resort to murder to get what they want. The only thing they understand is money, and they have enough of that to get what they want legally."

"Maybe we weren't getting out fast enough for them!" the first man, Aaren Buchner, declared. "And it seems to me Jude Kingman made a point of talking to *you* more than once, Ingrid Svensson!

Was he sweet on you? Maybe he wasn't too crazy about you marrying Carl. They did get in a scuffle, remember. Maybe it was over more than the railroad." He stepped closer to Ingrid. "And maybe you had an eye for the man's money."

"You take that back!" Johnny barreled into Buchner, punching wildly.

"Stop it, Johnny!" Ingrid screamed.

Buchner pushed Johnny away, ducking and laughing until Albert pulled his son off the man.

"He shouldn't have said that!" Johnny yelled, nearly crying. His face was flushed with anger, looking even redder against his blond hair bleached lighter by the summer sun.

"Let it go, Johnny!" his father told him. "People are just upset. Carl vas such a good friend to all of these men."

Johnny shook off his father and stormed away, kicking at dirt and rocks as he headed back to town.

"Look vat has happened," Albert told the others. "Ve can prove nothing, nor can ve disagree that the railroad did not need to resort to violence. Whoever did this has to be truly evil, and although I do not call him friend, Mr. Kingman does not strike me as such an evil man, despite that he is vealthy and came here to order us off of our land. Every von of you knows Ingrid vell enough to realize that a man's vealth vould mean nothing to her. The next man who accuses her of going after a man for his money vill answer to *me*, not to Johnny! And when I am angry, you do not vant to be fighting me!"

"Far!" Ingrid protested.

"Never mind!" He waved Ingrid off. "Look at us! Are ve going to let this railroad thing destroy our friendships and our Christian beliefs in the goodness of man? I vill remind all of you that ve still have crops to get in, and ve just might need each other to help do that. For now ve have to concentrate on praying for rain, and talk about how ve might be able to save Carl's corn, too. He vould vant us to save it and to divide the profits among us so that some of us might possibly save our farms. That is all ve should be thinking about—and praying about."

Albert took Ingrid's arm and marched away with her.

"I am sorry, Far."

"For what? You have done nothing. You even tried to reason with that railroad man. I think you bought us more time by convincing him to give us until harvesttime to come and collect."

"I don't understand any of this. Poor Carl! I cannot get out of my mind the picture of him lying there. It keeps me awake at night."

"Time vill take care of that, daughter, and it vill also heal your heart. I do not understand his death, either, but ve must go on, just as I did after your mother's death."

"We must stay for the gathering at the town hall in Carl's memory. But now I worry about what will be said behind my back."

"Do not vorry. You know who your friends are, and they vill not feel any differently. The others do not matter." Albert began walking faster. "I vant to find Johnny and calm him down."

"But Far, what about *you*? How are you feeling—about Carl's death, the railroad, all of it? What if we do lose the farm?"

He stopped and faced her, and she could see the hurt in his eyes. "I am not sure. I try not to consider it. It is my life, Ingrid."

She grasped his hands. "We will survive, no matter what. All that is important is that we are all together, ya?"

He smiled sadly. "Ya. Now, let us find Johnny and talk to him. Then ve go to the gathering."

Chapter Fifteen

Ingrid sat alone in the church while her father and Johnny attended a meeting of the Grangers. She wanted the peace and quiet in the small structure that followed Sunday services, and time to reflect on all that had happened. Still haunted by how she'd found Carl and Stanley just a week ago, she prayed for the strength to live with the memory and with what the outcome of all of this might be. She could not help tears of loneliness and confusion, and she preferred to cry alone here, where Johnny would not see.

Because the culprit might be Jude, and because

she'd once been seen talking alone with him the day of the fight between Jude and Carl, some people she'd once called friends now shunned her.

Jude had made no appearance since that day they'd talked alone at her farm. His absence stirred only more anger and suspicion among Plum Creek's citizens, as well as terrible doubt in her own heart. A United States Marshal had come to Plum Creek to investigate the shootings, and at a town meeting he'd assured citizens that the railroad would also be thoroughly investigated in relation to the event. However, he highly doubted railroad involvement. As Connelley had mentioned, it would not have been necessary for them to commit such a heinous crime to get what they wanted. The courts would end up giving them what they wanted anyway, and they had the time and the money to wait for that. Ingrid wanted to believe that, because it would mean Jude had nothing to do with Carl's death.

The marshal believed someone probably intended to rob the Ungers and became angry when they found little to steal. His suggestion brought shouts and raised fists from those at the meeting who were fully convinced it was the railroad's doing, but most also agreed that even the best of investigators would be hard-pressed to find any concrete proof of railroad involvement.

She listened to the patter of rain against the church's tin roof. Finally they'd gotten their much-needed precipitation, but too little too late. It was just enough to send the corn stalks a little higher, but not enough to ensure fat, sweet kernels. And now corn borers were having a feast, so many that it was almost impossible to keep up with them by picking off the affected ears or even cutting down whole stalks. Without the help of Carl and his father, much of Ingrid's own yield would be lost.

She sat there trying to understand why God had brought such a plague of bad luck on her family and the whole town, and especially Carl. What had any of them done wrong to deserve this? She didn't want to be angry with God. She just wanted to understand, and oddly, as she quietly prayed for that understanding, a voice spoke up behind her.

"Hello, Ingrid."

Startled, she turned to see Jude standing just behind her pew. "Jude!"

He smiled. "You aren't carrying a gun, are you?"

"I—" Ingrid quickly looked around, wiping at her tears as she did so. "You should not be here! The whole town blames you for Carl and Stanley Unger's deaths."

"I am well aware of that. All I care about is

what *you* think. May I sit down?" He nodded toward her pew.

Ingrid scooted over, realizing that during her prayers Jude Kingman had shown up as though sent by God. To think of it that way would be humorous if not for the gravity of the situation. "So much has happened!" she explained as he removed his hat and sat down beside her. "We are losing our corn to drought and corn borers. We are losing everything." She looked away, feeling ridiculous admitting her devastation in front of the man who was responsible for her troubles. She took a deep breath against more tears. "You must think me quite foolish to be complaining to you, of all people."

He sighed, leaning back in the pew. "Actually, I'm just relieved to be halfway welcomed by you, after all that's happened, especially regarding Carl. I am sincerely sorry about that, Ingrid, and I tell you honestly that I had absolutely nothing to do with it. I came here to tell the whole town just that, and to let them know I'm conducting my own investigation. That's why I've stayed away so long. I've been in Chicago asking questions. Please tell me you believe me when I say I am not responsible for what happened to Carl."

"I wondered, like everyone else, but Far and I

both could not bring ourselves to believe you would do such a thing." She met his eyes and saw great relief there.

"Thank you," he said softly, looking very tired and sad.

How she wished the man was less attractive, or meaner, more arrogant and uncaring. It would be so much easier then to convince herself she cared nothing about him, easier to hate and distrust him, as well she should.

"How did you get into town and into this church without being noticed, Jude? It is very dangerous for you to be here."

He put an arm across the back of the pew. "Oh, I came with plenty of men in case I need them. They're waiting in a plain, unmarked passenger car. I didn't want to attract attention by arriving in my private Pullman. I had the train let me off outside of town and I took back alleys and such to get to the church, although I was able to come in right through the front door without being noticed. I did see several men gathered down at the livery."

"Yes, another meeting of the Grangers," Ingrid told him with a sigh. "I did not want Far to go, but right now emotions are running high. You were wise not to let yourself be seen by that bunch without guards." He looked so utterly handsome, not at all cruel or heartless. "Why did you even take the chance? And what possessed you to come here to the church? How did you know I would be here?"

He smiled, looking suddenly a bit bashful and nervous. "Want the truth?"

"The truth is always best."

He did it again—looked her over in that special way that unnerved her. Then he turned to face forward, leaning to rest his elbows on his knees. "Believe it or not, Ingrid, I thought I might try some of my own praying. I, uh, I have certain personal problems that I don't quite know what to do about. And the way you have of bravely facing adversity and seeming to—I don't know—seeming to want to do the right thing no matter what... I've thought about that. And I realized your faith must have a lot to do with it." He straightened and faced her again. "I envy people like you, people who know exactly where they stand when it comes to right and wrong and who have principles. Where I come from, those things don't matter much. I just thought I'd come here and think about all of that, about what direction to take in my own life. And when I'm here I feel closer to you. I didn't know you'd stayed after church, but the fact that you did is a very pleasant coincidence."

She felt her cheeks warming. "Perhaps it's not a coincidence at all."

He frowned. "What do you mean?"

"It's just…" She looked down at the handkerchief crushed in her hand. "Perhaps God brought you here for a purpose. I was praying about what has happened, and actually praying you had nothing to do with Carl's death, and then, there you were."

He smiled softly. "So, you believe things happen because of God's doing?"

She returned the smile, feeling a little better. "Yes, I do. Maybe He even caused your father to make the decision to send you here. Maybe God *wanted* you here."

"Oh? For what?"

She shrugged. "Maybe for this moment, to awaken you to prayer and make you see you need Him in your life."

"And maybe to meet you and fall in love?"

Ingrid sat motionless as his arm came around her shoulders. She was so astonished at his remark that she could not meet his eyes. "Surely you can't mean that."

"I do mean it, Ingrid. I haven't been able to get you off of my mind since I first set eyes on you."

She scooted away. "I cannot talk of such things right now. My heart still aches for Carl's suffering. It isn't right to be discussing—discussing such a ridiculous suggestion."

"Ridiculous?"

"That you might love me. Our worlds could not be more different." Her heart pounded so hard she feared he might actually hear it.

"Tell me you don't have any feelings for me whatsoever, Ingrid, and I will go away and never come back."

Ingrid swallowed, her eyes tearing. "I—I do have feelings for you, but not feelings of love. That would be wrong."

"Why?"

His pressing questions were making her nervous, and too aware of his presence so close to her. "You know why. After Carl, and the farm, and all that you stand for, what would people think?"

"You nearly married a man you didn't love because you worried about what people might think. Follow your heart, Ingrid. I'm beginning to believe that's all that matters in life. I never had these feelings for any woman before I met you, and I have to tell you, you present a real challenge for me. I am not accustomed to women being put off by me and consistently turning me down."

Ingrid could only hope to find the right words. "We are just too different," she reminded him. "And right now I have my father and Johnny to think about, and the feelings of others. I truly do believe you have much in your personal life to pray about, Jude, things I know nothing about and would probably have trouble understanding. You need to set priorities for how you will use your wealth and power before you speak of love to a woman like me." She looked away.

He leaned back and rubbed his neck as though weary. "The way I was raised, maybe I don't even know what love is," he said sadly.

She felt sorry for him at the remark. "One day it will become very clear to you, Jude, once God is truly in your life," she suggested, facing him again. "Just the fact that you came to this little church in the midst of a world outside that hates you shows me that you think of God as your refuge, which He truly can be." She reached over and dared to take his hand. "Maybe someday, weeks or months from now, we can talk again, when all this is over and Johnny and my father and I are settled wherever we will be. Maybe then you will have resolved the things that make you so unhappy and we can..." She looked down, embarrassed. "We can talk."

He squeezed her hand, scooting closer and capturing her gaze. "I look forward to that day," he said. "I know this is a bad time for you, Ingrid. It's a bad time for me, too. I'll take care of business here and go, but I'll be back. I won't be able to stay away from you."

His continued vows of affection astonished her, and when he leaned closer, she was too startled to object, nor did she pull away when he kissed her cheek lightly. "I truly believe I love you, Ingrid."

"Jude—"

"Don't say a thing. I'm just glad you believe me when I say I had nothing to do with Carl's death. And I'm glad you're calling me Jude. I feel as though I've gained a great deal of ground just getting that much from you." He smiled gently, then squeezed her hand once more before rising. "I guess I'd better get out of here before you're seen consorting with the enemy again."

Ingrid stood up to face him. "I no longer think of you that way, Jude. I cannot say that I love you, but I most certainly do not hate you."

He picked up his hat and put it back on. "Well, with all that's going to take place the next few weeks I'll be staying completely out of your life, so I guess I'll say goodbye for now. I am so glad you were here so I could talk to you once more and see in your eyes that you believe me about Carl."

She touched his arm. "Jude, you said you came here to pray. If you want me to leave—"

"My prayers have already been answered. I

found you here and cleared the air over Carl's death. That's all I really hoped for. Now I have the doubtful, and likely dangerous, task of explaining myself to the town of Plum Creek."

"I am truly sorry all the blame for Carl's death is falling on you."

He smiled, but she saw the sadness in his dark eyes. "It's to be expected. I hope things will go well for you and your family, Ingrid. I want very much to help you, but you won't allow it, and I understand and respect that. For now I have some investigating as well as some explaining to do. I'll be back later with several of my men to hold a meeting. It might be best if you weren't even there."

She nodded. "I understand."

He sighed, looking her over again lovingly. "Goodbye, Ingrid."

Their eyes held, and she suspected he wanted to embrace her. She turned away. "Goodbye, Jude. Be careful."

She felt his hand on her shoulder, and he gently squeezed it reassuringly. Then she heard his footsteps as he left her and headed up the aisle to the front entrance. She heard the door open and close.

Ingrid closed her eyes, thinking there was such a loneliness about the man that she wanted to reach out and embrace him.

Suddenly she heard the startling crack of gunfire. She gasped, then turned and ran to the church entrance, flinging open the door. There at the bottom of the steps lay a man, bleeding and groaning. Rain poured down on him, creating a red stream that trickled over the ground. He rolled over, grasping his side.

"Jude!" she whispered.

Chapter Sixteen

Ingrid rushed to kneel beside his body. Jude lay
curled on his left side, his vest and outer coat
stained with blood. He groaned again, muttering
her name.

"I am right here, Jude!" she told him, going to
her knees beside him. She removed her cape and
laid it over him. "Oh, Dear Lord, please do not let
this man die!"

Several people came running, including Ingrid's
father and a farmer named George Connelley.
"What has happened here?" Albert demanded.

"Mr. Kingman was walking out of church when

someone shot him!" Ingrid nearly screamed, tears coming to her eyes over the sheer ugliness of the situation. "How could someone do something like this? He isn't even armed!"

"Same way someone could shoot down Carl and his pa!" Connelley replied.

Sheriff Jared Proctor arrived on the scene, panting from running. "What the—"

"No one deserves this!" Ingrid shouted to Connelley. "Nct Carl or his father, and not Mr. Kingman, either." She looked around at the gathering crowd. "Someone help me get Mr. Kingman to the doctor!"

The armed men who'd accompanied Jude came running from the train depot. One cussed when he saw it was Jude who'd been shot. "I told him he should have let us come with him!" Ingrid recognized the man as the broad-shouldered guard Jude called Benjamin.

"He didn't want the attention just yet," another said. "He insisted on going alone to the church first."

Benjamin removed his woolen suit jacket and threw it over Jude for more protection against the rain. "Let's get him onto the train and take him to Omaha," he suggested. "There's no doctor around here who'd be good enough to treat Mr. Kingman. I sure don't want to answer to his father if he dies."

"No!" Ingrid protested, rain soaking her hair and dress. "You have no idea how badly he is hurt. He could die if he does not at least have his wound dressed first. He is losing blood even as we speak."

"Who are you?" one of Jude's men asked.

"She's Ingrid Svensson," Benjamin told him.

It struck Ingrid that apparently Jude had talked to him about her. "We have a perfectly good doctor here," she pleaded with Benjamin. "Let him at least see if he can stop the bleeding first."

"Let him bleed to death," George Connelley sneered. "He's bleeding *us* to death."

"*You* did this, didn't you?" Ingrid said, glaring at George, a man she and her father once called friend.

Connelley frowned. "No! But I sure thought about it."

"Calm down, Ingrid," Proctor told her. "We'll get to the bottom of this."

Just then someone shouted, looking up and pointing. "There he is!"

On a rooftop across the street someone ducked away.

"Looks like Gunter Sternaman!" Connelley yelled. Some of Jude's men took off running.

"Hey, you stay out of this!" Proctor called to them.

"Try and stop us!" one of them shouted in reply. Proctor sprinted after them.

"Stop arguing and get this man to the doctor!" Ingrid again demanded.

"What are *you* doing involved in this, Ingrid?" The question came from Plum Creek's livery owner, Ted Hiler.

"Yeah!" others chimed in.

"We've seen you with Kingman more than once," Hiler pointed out. "What's going on between you two?"

"That is enough of that!" Albert spoke up in defense of his daughter. "You vill not speak that way about my Ingrid."

"I don't care about any of that!" Ingrid shouted. "We've left this man lying here long enough. Every minute counts. Please get him to the doctor."

"You men break this up and make room," Benjamin ordered. "Somebody get that wagon over there and put Mr. Kingman in it. We'll haul him over to the doctor right away. The doc sure can't do anything with him lying here in the rain. He'll take sick!"

A man hurried over to Ingrid's wagon, which was hitched nearby. He brought it over, and four men picked Jude up and carefully laid him in the back of the wagon. Ingrid climbed in with him, relieved that the rain had suddenly and abruptly stopped. In spite of the warm day, she shivered from her wet hair and clothes.

"Ingrid!" her father spoke up. "What are you doing?"

"I am going with him," she declared.

"Ingrid—" Albert shook his head "—it does not look good."

"I am tired of worrying about how things look!" she told him, fighting an urge to burst into tears. She glanced around at the others. "Many of you were not even going to bother getting help for this man. What was once a peaceful Christian community is turning into a place of hatred and unconcern for others! Look how easily Satan enters your hearts, making a good man like Gunter Sternaman try to *murder* someone!"

Benjamin climbed into the driver's seat and whipped the horses into motion.

"Two blocks down on the right," Ingrid shouted to him. She moved her arms under Jude's head to cradle it as the wagon splashed and bounced along the muddy street. She could only pray that Doctor Alwood would be able to help Jude. At least she knew he cared only about helping the sick, whether rich or poor, good or bad.

She fought feelings of horror and confusion. Her father was right in wondering what others would think of her being in the church alone with Jude Kingman, no matter how circumstantial and innocent. And much as she should not care about this man, her heart pounded with dread that he might die. How strange that if he did, she would miss him just as much, or more, than she missed Carl.

Jude reached up and grasped one of her arms, and Ingrid agonized over the violent bouncing of the simple farm wagon. Jude's grip tightened on her arm, as though only she could help him cling to life.

She looked back to see the rest of Jude's men dragging Gunter Sternaman toward the jailhouse. Sheriff Proctor was with them.

The whole world seemed upside down. Good people doing ugly things, a supposedly "bad" person showing a goodness no one knew about, and the man she'd nearly married lying in his grave, possibly murdered by associates of the man who now clung to her for support.

They reached the doctor's office, and Dr. Alwood, a graying man with an abrupt personality, ordered Kingman's men to get Jude inside quickly and lay him on a table covered with a clean sheet.

"Get these wet clothes off him!" the doctor ordered. "If he doesn't die from the gunshot wound, he'll die from pneumonia!"

Ingrid looked away as the doctor and others quickly stripped off Jude's clothes. She thought she heard Jude mumble something as Alwood began spouting more orders to his wife, who was a nurse. He asked three of the men to hold up extra lanterns so he could see better, and as he probed the wound, Jude let out a spine-chilling cry of pain.

"Get some laudanum down him," Alwood told his wife. "The bullet isn't that deep. I think I can get it out right here and now."

Ingrid shivered from wet chills as she stood at the side of the room, watching the clock as Alwood continued working, Jude crying out intermittently. Ingrid wanted to help, but Alwood seemed to have plenty of assistants. She could only wait and pray.

"Are you sure you know what you're doing?" Benjamin asked Alwood.

"Of course I know what I'm doing!" Alwood snapped.

"What if the wound gets infected?"

"That won't be my fault! You should have got him here before he got so totally soaked!"

"I just don't want to answer to his father," Benjamin explained.

"Did anybody even wire Jefferson Kingman yet?" one of the others asked.

"The old man will have fits over this one," another put in. "He'll probably come down here and hang every farmer around Plum Creek."

There came light laughter.

"Leastways they'll get kicked out or burned out," another offered.

Such ugliness. Would Jude really allow such a thing? What was his father like, the man who would "kick out or burn out" every farmer in Plum Creek? What was it about Jude's family that caused him unhappiness? Jude lacked for nothing, yet he always seemed so troubled.

It was strange, she realized; they had not really talked that often, yet when they did, it felt as if they had always known each other.

She quietly prayed, listening to more doctor's orders, more deep groans from Jude.

"Don't die on us, boss," Benjamin said. "We'll all lose our jobs."

The men all chuckled again, and Ingrid sensed affection beneath the laughter. These men obviously liked and respected Jude Kingman.

When Ingrid finally glanced at a clock, she was surprised to realize that nearly an hour had passed since coming into the office.

"There it is," Doctor Alwood said.

Ingrid heard the plinking of the bullet hitting a porcelain pan.

"Good job, Doc," Benjamin told him.

"We still have to worry about infection, as you

pointed out. I'll douse plenty of alcohol into the wound before stitching it up. The rest is up to the Lord and this man's basic good health."

More groans came from Jude, and Ingrid felt sick. She longed to hold his hand and reassure him.

"Let's get this wrapped good and tight," the doctor said after several more minutes. A couple of Jude's men helped hold him up as the doctor and his wife worked with clean gauze, wrapping it around Jude's middle. Jude's continued cries tore at Ingrid's heart.

"Do we have a bed ready, Sarah?" the doctor asked his wife.

"Yes."

"He'll have to stay here. Wouldn't be a good idea to move him now," Alwood told Jude's men.

"He asked for Ingrid before you put him under, Doc," Benjamin told the man. "Maybe she should sit with him, if she's willing."

Alwood straightened, turning to face Ingrid. "Do you want to sit with him, Ingrid? You don't need to, you know. It won't look good."

Ingrid scanned all of them, seeing the questions in the eyes of Jude's men and the doctor. "Mr. Kingman could die. If staying with him could ease his pain, how can I turn him down? It would not be Christian." She rose. "And at the moment, Dr.

Alwood, I am not the least bit concerned about how things look. I will sit with Mr. Kingman."

Benjamin smiled at her. "Thank you, ma'am."

The men proceeded to carry Jude into a back room that served as a minihospital for people who couldn't make it to Omaha, and couldn't afford it even if they were able to travel. The men were careful to keep blankets wrapped around Jude, and while they got him into a bed, the doctor's wife came over to Ingrid with an extra blanket.

"You'll take sick yourself sitting there in those wet clothes, Ingrid. I can get you one of my dresses to change into, if you wish."

"No, thank you. I'll be fine. I do appreciate the blanket." Her neck stiff from tension, Ingrid pulled the blanket around herself as Jude's men tucked Jude in, leaving his bare arms and shoulders free. Ingrid felt somewhat embarrassed to see Jude without his shirt, but this was no time for protocol or bashfulness.

Benjamin put yet another blanket over Jude, this time pulling it to his neck. He ordered one of the other men to get over to the telegraph office and wire Jefferson Kingman. All but Benjamin left, and the broad-shouldered man turned to Ingrid then.

"Thank you for staying with him, Miss Svensson. He is actually a good man, you know."

Ingrid smiled. "I know."

"I can promise you, ma'am, that Jude had nothing to do with the Unger shootings. I'd be the one who'd know."

Ingrid nodded. "I believe you." She glanced at Jude. "Mr. Kingman has become a...a good friend. Heaven knows he has no others in this town. I am glad to sit with him."

Benjamin nodded. "The rest of the men and I will be at the train depot if we are needed. I'm sure his father will be here within a day or so."

The man left, and Doctor Alwood pulled a chair close to the cot so Ingrid could sit down. "Do you want anything, Ingrid—some hot tea, perhaps?"

Nothing seemed real. "Yes, that would be very nice."

Alwood left, and a bewildered Ingrid stared at a now-unconscious Jude. The reality of what had happened set in then, along with a feeling of helplessness and hopelessness. She sat down, taking Jude's hand in her own and praying for him, for Plum Creek, for her family, for Gunter Sternaman, and asking for help with her own confused feelings.

The tears flowed, and when she finished and straightened, she noticed a tray with a pot of tea and a cup sitting on a table beside Jude's cot. She'd not even realized someone had brought it in.

Chapter Seventeen

Ingrid rubbed her eyes at the sound of voices outside Jude's room. She realized it was dawn. She'd
slept in the chair beside Jude's bed all night. She
stood up and stretched as she tucked some loose
hairs back into her bun. The door burst open then,
startling her.

Two men entered the room, and both stopped
in their tracks at the sight of her. She assumed
they must be Jude's father and brother, though
neither looked like Jude in the least. The father
was not as handsome nor as tall as Jude. The
brother was even shorter and resembled his father

in features and in the coloring of his sandy hair and blue eyes. Both were dressed in obviously expensive suits, gold watch chains hanging from satin brocade vest pockets, hair slicked back beneath silk hats.

"You're Ingrid Svensson?" the brother asked.

Ingrid held up her chin proudly. "I am."

He looked her over as though she were trash and snickered. "So, the milkmaid is moving in on the rich man."

"That's enough, Mark," Jude's father ordered.

Ingrid could just imagine their thoughts—a peasant woman sitting with their esteemed family member.

"I am Jefferson Kingman," the older man told her, "and this is my son Mark." He spoke the words as though he expected her to be highly impressed.

"You did not have to tell me who you are," she answered, standing her ground. "I knew you would come. Jude will be fine, according to the doctor."

"We'll get our own doctor's opinion on that," Mark told her, literally shoving her aside to move around to the other side of the bed. "And the man who did this will pay dearly."

Ingrid folded her arms. "Like the farmers who have already been killed for fighting the railroad?" Ingrid asked, instantly regretting the words. The look that came into Mark Kingman's eyes made her want to wilt.

"You have no proof the railroad had anything to do with that," the young man practically snarled.

"You can leave now, Miss Svensson," Jefferson told her. "We'll take care of things from here on. We'll be taking Jude back to Chicago."

"The doctor said it would be better if he was not moved yet," she reminded him.

"I guarantee he'll be handled with the utmost care, and he'll certainly get the best attention once he's in a *real* hospital."

Ingrid did not miss the emphasis on the word *real*. She could tell it would be useless to ask to go along, but she knew instinctively that Jude would want to wake up to find her there. Once last night, after rousing for a brief moment, he'd been too weak to speak, but the look on his face had told her he was glad she was there. Since then he'd slept again from more laudanum.

"Your son wants me with him," she dared tell the senior Kingman.

The man grinned and looked her over as though she were a lowly servant. "Tell me, Miss Svensson, how did you manage to get under Jude's skin, other than with your beauty, I mean?"

Mark chuckled. "Jude never could resist a beau-tiful woman, no matter what her station in life."

Ingrid would not allow the remark to hurt. That was what they wanted, for her to think all Jude cared about was her looks, as though it certainly couldn't be anything more than that.

"My beauty?" she asked, her dislike for both men rapidly building. She reminded herself to be-have as a decent Christian woman should. "Why, thank you, Mr. Kingman," she told him, pretend-ing to be unaffected by his remark, "but I do not know what you mean by getting under Jude's skin. We are at best enemies who have found a way to get along." She turned to Mark. "In spite of his rea-son for coming here, your brother has been every bit the gentleman, which you seem to have trouble doing. You will take him away with you now, and that is to be expected. I may never see him again, but I will pray for him, as he asked me to do."

"*Pray* for him?" Mark laughed darkly. "Well, now, aren't you the smart-mouthed, disrespectful little wench!" He looked at Jefferson. "Father, I think we'd better get Jude back to Chicago and into the world he came from before he forgets he's a Kingman and ends up wearing overalls and carry-ing a pitchfork."

The elder Kingman chuckled, his eyes still on

Ingrid. "Perhaps we should." He folded his arms, looking Ingrid over with pity. "I must say I have to admire your boldness, Miss Svensson, but I assure you, if you knew Jude well you'd know that if he's given you any indication whatsoever that he is interested in you, it's all a front. There are only two things he's interested in—getting you off your farm, and perhaps getting you into a compromising situation. Be that as it may, I sent my son down here on a mission as a sort of test, and you have run him completely off course. If I'd known one of the farmers had such a beautiful daughter, I might have thought twice about sending Jude down here. As Mark told you, Jude has a weakness for pretty women, and they certainly have a weakness for him. You've been very clever in using your wiles to try to win him over to your side."

Now Ingrid folded her arms authoritatively, deciding that if this man wanted to spar with words, she was not going to back down. "I have done nothing of the kind, Mr. Kingman. And if you think I have some kind of intentions toward your son, you are entirely wrong. I simply care about him as a person, in spite of his reasons for coming here. And Jude is a far more decent and caring man than you give him credit for. After meeting you and his brother for these few short minutes, I think that now I understand why he is such a troubled, unhappy man. Good day, Mr. Kingman." She picked up her bag and walked past the man, her heart secretly aching at not being able to stay with Jude.

Maybe it was better this way. She was letting her heart run away with her. After meeting Jude's father and brother, it was more obvious than ever that she could never fit into their world, not as Jude's friend, and certainly not as anything more.

No one was in the office as she walked through it, but when she went outside, she found Dr. Alwood on the front stoop talking with her father, who stiffened when he saw Ingrid.

"Far, you stayed all night?"

He looked upset. "As you did."

"It was the Christian thing to do. There was not one other person in this town who cared if Mr. Kingman lived or died."

"Come. Ve vill talk on the vay home, not in front of the doctor. And you are a mess! You must get home and change."

Ingrid followed her father to the wagon, glad to go home where she could wash up and change her clothes. "Where is Johnny?"

"I sent him home yesterday vit the Murphys. They have to go by our place anyvay, and after the mess with the shooting and all, Leonard vanted to get his family home." They climbed into the wagon and Albert picked up the reins, urging the horses into a fast trot.

Ingrid noticed her father, too, was still wearing the clothes he'd worn to church yesterday morning. Now all of that seemed like such a long time ago, the shooting so unreal. "Why are you angry with me, Far? I have done nothing wrong."

"I know, but the others—now I am left having to try to explain my daughter's behavior."

"Behavior? Meeting Mr. Kingman in the church was a complete accident, Far. I cannot help it if he walked in while I was there. And it was a *church*, not a saloon or a private meeting at his train car."

"Surely you see it looked planned. After so many people seeing you talking alone vit that man after that ruckus in church a few veeks ago—it just all looks so bad, Ingrid. I am not blaming you for anything. I am just telling you how it looks. Besides that, I have seen your eyes. There is something there whenever you talk about Jude Kingman. In the name of our Good Lord, Ingrid, how can you have von speck of interest in a man like that, a man who comes from the kind of vealth ve could never understand, a man from a vorld vere they spit on people like us?"

Ingrid looked away. "I never once said I was interested in him in that way. I am not that stupid, and I still mourn poor Carl. You know that."

"Ah, Carl. His death being so recent only adds to the gossip—you being seen with the very man who could be responsible for it all." He shook his head.

"Far, not long ago you told me you did not believe Jude could do such a thing. You said you believed he was not such an evil man."

"That I did. I am telling you how *others* see it, not I. And, my girl, just because I said I did not see evil in him, that did not mean I thought you should befriend him. It did not mean ve have to like him, or even that he is not capable of cheating others to save his vealth. And speaking of evil, I *do* see it in his father and his brother. That is a family it vould be best to avoid."

Ingrid shivered at the memory of how the other two Kingmans had looked at her. "I agree."

They bounced along the roadway for several more minutes without speaking. At one point Ingrid looked back to see Jude Kingman's silk top hat still lying in the back of her wagon. For some reason the sight of it brought pain to her heart.

"Far."

"Yes, daughter."

"Isn't it sad that only Jude's father and brother came to get him, to see how he was doing? Why not his mother? Doesn't it seem that it would be the mother who would come first, flying to her son's side, even when her son is a grown man?"

Albert stared ahead. "I suppose."

Again there came silence for a few minutes. Ingrid thought about the day Jude changed the subject when she mentioned his mother. After meeting the father and brother, she couldn't help wondering what the mother was like. Her heart felt heavy for Jude. She suspected she felt more love from a mother who'd been dead for years than Jude Kingman felt from a mother who still lived.

Chapter Eighteen

August 18

Jude opened his eyes and looked around, taking a moment to realize he was in his own room in his wing of the Kingman mansion in Chicago. He lay gathering his thoughts, not able to remember at first why he was there—and in so much pain. He saw movement to his left and turned his head to see one of the housekeepers, Freida Banner, laying a silk robe over the back of a deep red velvet love seat. Although Freida was a stout German woman, just seeing another female brought Ingrid instantly to mind.

"Freida, where is Ingrid?"

The graying woman glanced at him, her aging face still smooth and tight, due partly to the way she wore her hair pulled back so severely into a bun that it seemed to stretch the skin of her face. "Ingrid? I don't know anyone called Ingrid, sir."

Jude looked around the room again. "How did I get here, of all places? Last I knew I was lying in a bed in some doctor's office in Plum Creek. And all I remember before that is walking out of a church and feeling terrible pain. Both times Ingrid was there."

Freida frowned as she stepped closer and tucked the covers around him. "It is good to see you awake, Mr. Kingman. All I can tell you, sir, is that two days ago you were shot in some little town in Nebraska. A doctor there took out the bullet, and your father and brother went to get you and brought you here by train last night. They decided you could heal just as well in your own bed as in a hospital, but they did bring in the family doctor, who told them everything looks fine. You have been on pain medicine the whole time. The doctor said you should be up and around in about a month." She walked over to pour some water from a pitcher into a glass on the stand beside his bed. "Your father hired a nurse to keep an eye on you for the next several days. I will go and tell her you are awake." She turned to leave.

"Wait!" Jude called out.

The woman turned.

"My brother and father brought me here?"

"Yes, sir."

"Did they say anything about a woman named Ingrid? Did they maybe bring her along?"

Freida shook her head.

Jude felt a terrible loneliness, realizing how nice it would have been to wake up to see Ingrid sitting here. "Don't fetch the nurse yet. Go get my father or Mark, if either of them is home."

"I will get Mark. He did not go to work today because all of you arrived so late."

Freida left, and Jude ran a hand through his hair, trying to think. Who had shot him? Obviously any number of men in Plum Creek probably wanted to. He shifted in his bed, grimacing at the pain in his side and understanding why he'd been kept on laudanum. It seemed strange to wake up here in Chicago when only two days ago he'd been sitting in a little church in Plum Creek...talking to Ingrid.

The memory brought a warmth to his insides and eased his pain. He loved her. She believed it was just his loneliness talking, but he was sure his feelings were real. She was so easy to talk to, so beautiful, so caring, so much a better person than anyone else he'd known. And she seemed to have more concern for him than did his own mother, who apparently had not even bothered to look in on him yet. He thought how, right now, he'd rather be in Plum Creek near Ingrid than lying here in luxury.

He looked up then to see Mark come into the room. After their last meeting in Omaha, Jude was not exactly excited to see his brother, but he needed some questions answered. The whole matter of the farmers and the railroad had got out of hand, and he'd promised Ingrid he would look into Carl's murder.

"Well, well, big brother, you're actually awake and talking," Mark said with mock concern. "Mother and Father will be thrilled."

"Where are they?"

"Father, of course, is at the office downtown. And this is Mother's day to hostess a university fund-raiser. She looked absolutely ravishing when she left."

"I'm sure she did. Did she bother to look in on me first?"

"No, but she did ask about you."

"How kind of her." Jude rubbed his eyes. "Tell

me something. Why did you and Dad bother to bring me all the way back to Chicago? You could have left me at the hospital in Omaha, since I take it my injuries are not life-threatening at this point."

Mark shrugged. "Just seemed the best thing to do. If there are people in Plum Creek who'd like to see you dead, there might be some in Omaha, too. The farther away, the better."

"Who shot me?"

"They think it was some German man named Gunter Sternaman."

Jude looked up at the fancy chandelier that decorated the room's high ceiling. "I might have guessed."

"Well, big brother, they're all up in arms over the shooting of that Unger fellow and his father."

Jude moved his gaze back to Mark. "Speaking of which—" He groaned with a sudden stab of pain in his side. "Everybody in Plum Creek thinks the railroad is involved in those murders," he continued, fighting the pain. "What do *you* know about it?"

Mark grinned. "What do *I* know? What is that supposed to mean?"

Jude wished he was stronger. "You know what it means. I've questioned everyone but you, and that's only because you so conveniently left Chicago on business right after those murders. Do you have any idea who might be responsible for the deaths of those men?"

Mark put up his hands. "All I know is that you went down there and created a mess by not taking care of matters the right way. Father is not at all pleased. He's put me in charge."

"Is that so?" Jude fought an urge to laugh because it would hurt too much. "That's the worst thing he could do. If those men want to see *me* dead, how do you think they'll feel about you if you go down there and use guns to force them out?"

"At least they will be gone."

"I'll talk to Father about that. Doing it your way will never work and will end up making *all* of us look bad, the railroad and the government. Leave it alone, Mark. And no matter what you do, I don't want anyone bothering Ingrid Svensson and her family. Leave them be and at least let them have their harvest."

He saw an ugliness move into Mark's eyes. "Ingrid Svensson is no different from the rest of them."

"Yes, she is. You bother her and you'll have me to answer to."

Mark's face reddened slightly. "Get over her, Jude." He nearly growled the words.

Jude frowned with a sudden realization. "She's

why you and Father brought me all the way back to Chicago, isn't she?"

A smirk came across Mark's face. "It's for your own good."

"What did you say to Ingrid? Were you rude to her?"

"On the contrary. *She* was rude to *us*, you might say."

Jude couldn't help a smile. "She stood up to you, did she?" He closed his eyes. "She's a proud woman, and I have a feeling you two did not intimidate her in the least."

Mark's eyes darkened. "Forget about her, Jude. She's a foreigner. Her accent is so strong you can hardly understand her, and she obviously knows nothing about the way we live. She'd be an embarrassment to you *and* to us. All she knows is farming. She certainly has no right being so uppity with people like father and me."

"Uppity? I have a feeling you two treated her in a way that gave her every right to be uppity." Jude couldn't help his anger. "You're just jealous because she's more beautiful than any woman either of us has seen here in Chicago."

Mark rolled his eyes. "Why mess around with a farm girl, Jude, when you have so many beautiful women right here in Chicago at your beck and call? Apparently that Swedish wench has barely done more than talk to you, let alone hold your hand or, heaven forbid, let you work your charms on her. She's as cold as ice, and unrefined. I have a feeling she wouldn't want any more to do with this family than we would with her, so rest up there, big brother. When you're healed, Father will give you something to do here in Chicago. Leave the farmer problem to me."

Much as it hurt, Jude managed to use his hands to shift to a sitting position. "Do you mind fixing the pillows behind me so I can lean against them?"

Mark did as he asked, though obviously peeved at having to do such a menial task, even for his own brother. He leaned over to fluff the pillows behind Jude, and that gave Jude the perfect chance to grab the front of his brother's shirt and jerk him close. He fought the crippling pain that engulfed him, but was determined to set things straight here and now.

"*I'll* go back to Nebraska and finish what I started!" he growled at Mark. "I don't want you going back there, or going anywhere near Ingrid Svensson. And one more thing—I'd better never find out you had something to do with Carl Unger's death."

Mark managed to pull away. "Apparently you are healed better than we thought," he said.

"Not really," Jude replied, glowering. He was bathed in sweat from pain. "I'm just mad enough to ignore the pain it takes to get my point across! Did you pay someone to kill Carl Unger and his father?"

Mark grinned nervously. "If I did, you can bet I'd pay him well—well enough that he'd be far away from here by now, never suspected and never found. and living like a king in California or maybe Mexico or Alaska." He stiffened. "Now, if you want to accuse me of having something to do with those murders, *prove* it!" He held out his hands. "My hands are clean, Jude."

Jude stared at him for a long, quiet moment. "I see blood on them."

Mark shrugged, his eyes narrowing. "See what you want. Proving it is impossible. And even if it *were* possible, things would only be worse. You would carry the same shame as anyone else with the Kingman name, let alone the possibility of causing an all-out war between farmers and the railroad, with more innocent lives lost. It's pointless to try to prove anything." He retucked his shirt and straightened his jacket. "It's time to just go on with life, Jude, the way it used to be. I've already had a couple of very lovely young women ask me how you are doing, both of whom would love to come in here and fuss over you. Take advantage of the situation." He put on a false smile. "You have become a bit of a hero, you know, going down there and facing those violent farmers and getting shot and all that. Why go back out there when your life is in such danger?"

"Because there is someone there I need to talk to. And I intend to ask the powers-that-be to let Gunter Sternaman go. I intend to forgive him."

"*Forgive* him!" Mark laughed loudly. "Please tell me you're *joking, Jude.*"

"It will give me a chance to mend things and keep the peace," Jude answered seriously. "Sternaman was just a man desperate to keep something he loves more than life itself. And if he shot me because he thinks the railroad had something to do with Carl Unger's death, I suspect he had a right, seeing as how it very likely *was* a railroad man who shot him, paid by you!"

Mark shook his head. "You are the biggest fool I have ever known. If you aren't careful, Jude, Father will cut you out of Kingman Investments altogether. If you intend to go after that Swedish peasant, maybe you'd better get used to living as she does, because that's just how you might end up."

"You'd like that, wouldn't you—to be the only one to inherit everything?"

Mark backed away. "Get some rest, Jude. Maybe sleep will help you think more clearly." He turned and left, and Jude laid his head back, his mind swimming with disappointment and dismay. He had no doubt Mark had something to do with those murders—his own brother, more evil than he'd ever dreamed.

Too much was starkly apparent. Mark was right in saying Jude would never be able to prove who killed Carl. And now he knew why his father and Mark were in such a rush to come down to Plum Creek and take him home. It wasn't so much out of love and concern as it was just to get him out of there and away from Ingrid, the woman who would embarrass the whole family if Jude ever brought her home with him.

But that wasn't what hurt the most. He had to face the fact that he was in love with Ingrid, a love that probably could never be returned in the way he'd like. In spite of all his money and power, the woman was far too good for him in too many ways to count.

Chapter Nineteen

Jude walked slowly back to bed, having managed to shave by himself. After waking up to reality yesterday, he'd decided to waste no time in getting back on his feet. He hated having other people take care of personal matters for him, and he was determined to get back to business as soon as possible to keep Mark from going to Plum Creek.

Mostly he dreaded the thought of how Mark would treat Ingrid and her father. Until landing back home, Jude had almost forgotten how impossible a relationship with someone like Ingrid would be. Heaven forbid he should bring that beautiful, innocent, proud woman into this family.

He grimaced as he sat down on the bed, angry with himself for being tired from the simple act of getting up and shaving. At this rate he'd never be fully recovered in time to keep Mark from making more trouble for the good people of Plum Creek. He had his own ideas about how to soothe their anger, and as soon as he was able, he would talk to his father about it.

"Jude? Are you presentable?"

Jude rolled his eyes at the sound of his mother's voice. "Yes." He made sure his silk robe was properly covering him as Corinne came into the room.

"Jude, my poor boy! How are you feeling this morning?" The woman rushed over to grasp his face and give him a peck on the forehead. Even though it was early morning Corinne was already dressed in an expensive day dress and perfectly coiffed, with just the right amount of color on her cheeks. Her hair was twisted and pinned into beautiful, large curls, and her complexion looked unreal in its perfection. Jude thought how she almost never exposed herself to the sun and always wore gloves so that her hands were still milky smooth. He wondered if she'd ever got them dirty in her whole life. She rose to that board-straight posture of hers then and looked him over.

"You're freshly shaved," she commented. "Have you been up?"

"How kind of you to ask, Mother," he answered cynically. "I was wondering if I'd see you before I was completely recovered and leaving again."

She frowned. "Oh, Jude, you know I had that benefit yesterday. We raised a good deal of money. By the time I arrived home, I was so tired I went straight to bed. I knew you were doing fine and that you were certainly being well cared for."

"Yes, well, I forgot what a caring philanthropist you are."

She folded her arms. "Do I detect sarcasm in that remark?"

He grinned. "Yes."

She waved him off and turned to straighten a picture on the wall. "I knew Mark had looked in on you in my place, darling man. He gave me a full report, and if I thought for a moment that you'd take a turn for the worse, I would have come quickly to your side."

Would you really? "Tell me," he said aloud, "what if I told you that your darling Mark arranged for the murder of a couple of the farmers down at Plum Creek?"

She swiftly turned, putting her hands on her hips. "What a cruel thing to say about your brother! Mark would never do such a thing. I can't imagine where you got such an idea, or why you brought it up out of the blue when I've just come here to visit and to sit with you for a while. Whatever has gotten into you, Jude?"

He sighed. "I'm not even sure myself." Why bother telling her anything bad about Mark? Mark was her pride and joy.

"Well, I have an idea why you've come back a different man." She walked closer.

"Who told you I'm a different man?"

"Mark and your father both. They say you've been procrastinating in your duties, Jude, and I suspect it has something to do with that Swedish farm woman Mark told me about. Surely you aren't losing your heart to someone like that, are you?"

There it was: the real reason his mother had bothered to come and see him. "Someone like what? You've never even met the woman."

"No, but—well, she's a *foreigner*."

"If memory serves me right, pretty much every person living in this country today is a foreigner, so to speak. The only ones who aren't are the Indians."

She rolled her eyes in exasperation. "Where on earth are you coming up with these thoughts? You know what I mean, Jude. She wasn't *born* here, and Mark says her accent is very distracting. She has apparently never known anything but a farmer's life, and he says she has a farmer's hands, rough and somewhat weathered. And she spoke to him and your father quite flippantly." She sniffed. "As if she had the right."

Jude frowned, thinking how much better a person Ingrid was than his own mother. "I believe that just a moment ago, Mother, you implied I was a grown man who didn't need his mother. I'd guess that means I have a right to my own opinion about women and a right to care about whomever I want. And I will thank you to never again make rude remarks about Ingrid Svensson. And by the way, if you saw her for yourself, you'd know what an utterly beautiful woman she is. If she was gussied up like the snooty women you run with, she'd put them all to shame with her beauty, believe me."

"Oh, Jude," she answered with pain on her face. "Please don't tell me you have deep feelings for that woman. For goodness' sake, you could have your pick of any lovely, refined debutante in all of Chicago—or New York or Boston or Philadelphia, for that matter. You are a *most* handsome man, with the world at your feet. I'll say it again, it's time you married and gave us some grandchildren.

How I would love to help with a grand wedding held right here at the mansion in the ballroom." She spoke the last words with her eyes closed and a smile on her face.

"Is it required that I actually *love* this debutante, or do I just marry her for prestige? Maybe I should marry one so that we breed more gentlemen and debutantes who carry the proper bloodlines. Is that it?"

Angry disappointment suddenly shone in her eyes. "Why do you talk that way, Jude? I swear one would think you didn't even belong—" Her face suddenly flushed. "You behave as though you aren't even part of this family."

"Well, Mother, I don't always *feel* like part of this family. The older I get, the more I believe that ethics are as important in life as money."

"Ethics?" She let out an odd gasping laugh. "Are you saying this family has no *ethics*?"

The woman would never understand anything he was trying to say. She lived in a world of her own. He rubbed at his eyes wearily. "I am just saying that if and when I get married, it will be for love, not because she's rich and beautiful. I've had my fill of rich and beautiful women who are empty inside, who have no goal in life other than to marry a rich man and worry about the latest fashions."

"Don't think that Swedish woman isn't interested in marrying money! She has a plan, you can bet on it. And if you have even the tiniest thought of bringing her into this family, get rid of them now. It would never work. If you truly care about her, just remember how miserable someone like that would be living in our world. I can't think of one of our friends who would be kind to her, and the jealous young women in our circle who have tried to win you over would be horribly cruel to her."

Corinne turned and walked to the fireplace. "Dotty Karne and Susan Henderson have been wanting to visit you and see how you are. I'll let them know they can come tomorrow." She fussed with a picture on the fireplace mantel, then faced him. "You have become quite the hero, you know. Mark is terribly jealous. All the young ladies want to visit with the brave man who put his life in danger for the sake of Kingman Investments and as a duty to his father."

"That's ridiculous. And I can't think of one person in Chicago I'm anxious to visit with, including Dotty and Susan. Don't go inviting them here, because I would embarrass you by telling them to leave. Just go take care of your civic duties, Mother. I'll handle my recovery—and my life— the way I see fit."

A look of dark warning came into her eyes. "Then you just remember what I've told you about that Swedish woman."

"Her name is Ingrid Svensson. Quit calling her 'that Swedish woman.'"

"I do not want her setting foot in this house, Jude. Please don't embarrass me that way."

"Believe me, Mother, she wouldn't *want* to set foot in this house."

"And I never want to hear another word about Mark being responsible for someone's murder. That is a horrible accusation, Jude. To make it against your own brother makes it even worse."

She would never understand or accept the truth. "Just leave, Mother. I am suddenly very tired."

She blinked down at him. "Well, I'm sure you'll be fine, dear, and as soon as you are up and around and get used to being home again, you'll forget all about that woman and see her for what she really is, a poor, simple farm girl looking to get rich quickly by marrying into money."

Jude grimaced with pain. "Nobody said anything about marrying anyone. You have blown this all out of proportion, Mother."

"Good then. Sleep well, Jude."

Jude heard the rustle of her skirts as she left, heard the door quietly close. He was relieved that she was gone. Being around Corinne only made him long for Ingrid's soft voice, her lovely smile and the simple way she dressed and wore her hair.

He rested against the pillows again. The visit from his mother had worn him out.

Chapter Twenty

Early October

Ingrid's hands still ached from nearly two weeks of shucking acres of corn. The constant yanking and jerking down the stalks with her shucking gloves had taken its toll. The shanks did not always give way easily, and the hooks on the gloves needed constant sharpening.

The job of harvesting was finally complete, and today she wore pink gloves on her hands to cover the sad condition of her skin, always a problem after harvest. Following so much hard work it was a relief to wear one of her better dresses, a pink checkered one with a fitted bodice that showed off her slender waist. She'd decorated her straw bonnet with pink silk flowers.

The gloves helped her sore hands while holding the reins as she guided the two plow horses that pulled her wagon to Plum Creek. The corncribs at home were relatively full, considering the poor harvest. Buyers would soon come out to the farm with their offers, and the money from the corn, along with the farm equipment, her Concord range, the furniture and two crates of chickens in the back of the wagon, would help her and her father and Johnny settle in Omaha, where they would look for jobs. Today they would post flyers in town advertising the fact that all their stock and bigger equipment was also for sale.

The time had come to face reality. They would not have enough money to save the farm or even pay the taxes on it. What made her sadder yet was that she'd not heard a word from Jude in nearly six weeks. She wanted to see him again, just to be sure he was all right. His long absence was likely due to his recovery, but he could have written her, or wired.

So be it. It was best for both of them.

As she drove past the church steps she couldn't

help thinking about the awful day of the shooting, the horror of thinking Jude might die, the pleading in his eyes that she stay with him. All that had likely changed. His old way of life back in Chicago had by now reminded him of his foolishness in talking to her about love and courtship. She just wished she could understand why the Good Lord brought Jude into her life in the first place.

The situation in Plum Creek was now calmer, but because of the drought, two more farmers had given up and moved away, letting the railroad do whatever they planned with their farms.

It was over—all the years of hard work, joy of ownership, pride in success were over. Through prayer she'd asked God to give her the grace to accept what could not be changed, and to forgive those at fault. Her biggest worry now was her father, who'd gone from a proud farmer to an angry farmer to a determined man who'd decided he would somehow find work and keep the family going. But doing anything other than farming would be so hard for him, and he was still having back problems.

Johnny sat in the back of the wagon, still too young to understand the gravity of their situation and instead excited about the trip to town and the fact that Plum Creek was packed with farmers meeting with buyers. A few of those buyers had already headed out with large freight wagons to collect corn from cribs at other farms, corn that would be shipped by train to Chicago.

What a long, hard, hot summer it had been, a summer of so much discontent, not only in the community of Plum Creek, but in her own heart. The time had truly come to give up the farm. The reality of it was at times crushing.

"Hey, Albert!"

Ingrid slowed the wagon in front of Grooten's Dry Goods when Hans Grooten called out to her father. Ingrid braked the wagon.

"Hans!" Albert greeted. "Good to see you. I vanted to talk to you about buying some of my things for resale."

"Sure, but that's not why I called to you." Hans stepped closer. "That Jude Kingman is back in town—came here in his fancy Pullman with a whole army of men. He sent his men out to announce Kingman wants to hold a meeting at four o'clock at the town hall. Guess he figured with so many farmers in town this time of year, this would be a chance to tell them the time has come to get out."

"Wow!" Johnny exclaimed. "Maybe there will be a fight!"

"Johnny, do not talk that way!" Ingrid demanded. "You should pray there will be no trouble." Jude was here! Would he try to see her?

"I cannot believe that man came back," Albert muttered. "Kingman is probably here with lawyers to make sure Gunter gets vat is coming to him," he told Hans. "Maybe he vill even take Gunter back to Chicago and have him imprisoned there. It is shameful how long Gunter has sat in jail here vaiting for a trial." He climbed down from the wagon. "Tie the horses, Ingrid. I vill talk to Hans about buying our things. Johnny, you stay and help me unload."

Ingrid obeyed, climbing down and securing the horses to a hitching post in front of Grooten's. "I am going to walk over to the church, Far. There is much to pray about."

If Jude wanted to see her, he would have men watching out for her. He would want her to go where they could be alone...again.

"Ya, vit that Jude Kingman back in town, there is much to pray about," Albert commented.

Ingrid turned away. She must be losing her mind to be plotting a way to see Jude again! And here she'd just convinced herself it was best if that never happened. Where had all her common sense gone? All it took was the mention of Jude's name and her heart went racing again, while her sense of right and wrong vanished.

She hurried to the church, wanting to cry, hating Jude Kingman for making her feel so confused, yet somehow still wanting to see him again. She went inside, breathing deeply of the peace and quiet. Here she found a wonderful, soothing calm. She reasoned that she would have come here even if Jude was not in town. She missed church. Harvest had kept her away, but more than that, the cruel stares and gossip of others had kept her away. Moving to Omaha was not due just to losing the farm. They had lost good friends because of people's misunderstanding of her relationship with Jude. She was considered a traitor, and Ingrid did not want Johnny to grow up in a town where others would not be kind to him and might say cruel things.

She opened the front door and stepped inside, glad no one else was there...yet wishing one particular person might come. She walked to the front, kneeling at the prayer railing. Sometimes she wished she could stay here forever and sleep in God's arms and never have to worry about another thing in her life.

She bowed her head, asking God to help her know her own heart. Her feelings for Jude Kingman were so jumbled. Surely the only reason she wanted to see him again was to be sure he was all right. Because of the way he'd left town, wounded and unconscious, with her unable to stay with him through his pain, it just seemed as though they needed some kind of closure.

She fought tears as she prayed for the courage it would take to leave the farm and Plum Creek and all things familiar to start over someplace new, especially a city as big as Omaha. It was then she heard the door to the office behind the church altar open and close, and when she looked up, there stood Jude.

How handsome he looked, as always! He wore dark pants and a white shirt, his nearly black hair slicked back neatly. "Jude!" she exclaimed, rising. Why was she so happy to see him?

"Benjamin told me he saw you come in here." He stepped closer. "You look lovely in pink."

She felt a warmth in her cheeks. "Thank you." She looked him over. "You're so thin."

"Thanks to a gunshot wound that ruined my appetite, but it's coming back now that I'm healed."

"I'm so glad you're better. I was so worried, and I never heard from you."

He studied her. "I thought it best, but I've missed you, Ingrid."

She took a deep breath against her pounding heart. "Hans Grooten told us you were in town for a meeting. I suppose you're here to tell us the time has come to get off our land."

"Actually I'm here to settle the matter of Gunter Sternaman, but before I do that, there is something I need to talk to you about, and I want to apologize for the way my father and brother must have treated you when they came for me."

She nervously smoothed her dress. "They were just upset."

He smiled wryly. "Don't make excuses for their behavior." He walked closer and motioned for her to sit down in a front pew. He sat down beside her. "I didn't come back as soon as I would have liked...a few setbacks in my recovery, but I'm fine now, though still a little weak. Lying around did give me time to think, Ingrid, and once I managed to convince my brother to keep his nose out of Plum Creek I decided to let matters settle down a bit here before I returned. I've made some decisions, Ingrid, but more than anything I wanted to see you and explain why, in spite of things I told you when last we talked..." He sighed, leaning forward and resting his elbows on his knees. "Why it could never work between us."

For some reason she felt a pull at her heart. "I already know that. Our worlds—"

"It's not that. Ingrid, you are stronger, braver, more honorable than any woman I've known. I admire you very much. That's why what I have to say is so difficult. You're so—so moral and trusting and you have so much faith in God and, I believe, in the goodness of people. Then I come along and test that trust and faith, and now I have to tell you something that will sicken the moral part of you and will probably cause you to hate me all over again."

Ingrid frowned, keeping her hands clasped tightly in her lap. He seemed deeply disturbed, so full of sorrow and regret. "I don't understand—"

"Ingrid, I think I know who killed Carl—or at least who had a lot to do with it."

Her eyes widened with surprise. "Who? Have you told the police?"

He stared at the floor. "No. It wouldn't do any good."

"Why not?"

"Because…"

He leaned back, turning to meet her gaze. Ingrid saw a deep pain in his eyes.

"Because it was my brother."

Ingrid blinked in shock. "Your *brother*!"

"I can't prove it, but he as much as admitted he hired someone to kill Carl and his father. You can bet that Mark made sure the killer was paid well enough to get as far away from here as possible and start a new life. With so many men in the employ of Kingman Enterprises, let alone the shady, back-alley contacts my brother probably has, I can't even begin to guess who it might have been. I am not acquainted with the darker side of life in the way that Mark is. And with our family acquainted with practically every judge and man of prominence in Chicago and the Kingman name connected to all kinds of philanthropic causes—" he shook his head "—there isn't a person of any standing or power who would believe Mark Kingman did such a thing. And if I were the one to accuse him, that would make it all worse. Without proof there would just be a terrible scandal. I'd break my father's and mother's hearts and the public would see it as some kind of jealousy thing between the Kingman brothers, that I was making up lies to make Mark look bad. I'd lose my own validity in the business world and—well, I think you can see how impossible it all is."

He closed his eyes and turned away. "My brother is getting away with murder, and I can't do anything about it. I'm sorry, Ingrid. I also know it's something that would always be there between us, ruining any chance we have of any kind of decent relationship."

Ingrid thought a moment. Yes, she could picture the arrogant Mark Kingman hiring someone to kill any man who got in his way. "Jude, why are *you* sorry? You have done nothing wrong."

He let out a light laugh of disgust. "Just being related to Mark makes me feel like I was part of it, let alone that I was the one to come down here and start things in the first place."

"You were doing your job."

He rose, walking over to the prayer rail and facing a large cross on the wall behind the pulpit.

"Jude, you are not your brother," Ingrid told him, standing. "Nor are you anything like him. And only God can judge us. You can't worry that your brother will never be punished. He *will* be punished—by God—either in this life or in the next. What you need to do is ask God to help you forgive him, and to help you let go of this and give it over to God to take care of."

He hung his head. "I'm not sure I can do that."

"You can, and you must."

He faced her, tears in his eyes. "Either way, I've done enough to devastate your life. Knowing what Mark has done only makes it all worse. I don't want to do one more thing that could hurt you even more than you've already been hurt these past few months, and acting on my feelings *would* end up hurting you, believe me. I know how you'd be treated in my world, and I can't do that to you. I wish I'd met you at a better time, maybe in another life."

He took a deep breath, walking a few steps away. "I gave serious consideration to giving up my life as a Kingman, but this thing with Mark would just—I don't know—blood is blood, and I feel like mine is tainted. You're too good for that."

"Jude—"

He put his hand up. "Hear me out. Even if you have no feelings for me, I want you to understand. I have a lot of decisions to make about my life before I can be the kind of man who deserves to love someone as wonderful as you. To be honest, I'm not all that sure I even know how love is supposed to feel." He stepped closer again. "And, my dear, sweet Ingrid, until I know that, and get a few other things right in my life, I don't want to burden your life any more than it's already been burdened. And I sure don't want to risk hurting you more. I never, ever want to do that. But maybe, just maybe, if the day comes that I've straightened myself out, you might find it in your heart to care for me just a little."

Ingrid felt paralyzed by the torrent of feelings inside her. She took a breath and finally said, "I will pray for you, for I can see you are still confused and lonely. And you must pray, Jude. Give God your heart. Only then will you find the happiness you seek and begin to learn the true meaning of love."

He studied her sadly. "After the papers are signed for the railroad, where will you go? What will you do?"

"We plan to go to Omaha. Johnny can get better schooling there, and my father and I will look for jobs."

"I have an office in Omaha. There is a man there named Wilson Beyers. If you need any kind of help, you look him up. He'll get hold of me and—"

"No. That would only…" She turned away. "It might…force us to see each other again. If you believe this—whatever it is we share—if you believe it should end, then it should end."

There came a moment of silence. "It's best. I'm flat-out not good enough for you."

She turned to him in surprise. "You? Jude Kingman? Not *good* enough? How can a man of your standing say such a thing?"

"A man's worthiness has nothing to do with his monetary value, his importance in society or his education. It comes from something deeper, something you've always had and I've *never* had."

Ingrid stepped closer. "But you *are* worthy,

Jude. In God's eyes, *all* are worthy. I'm no better than you in any way. You are letting your brother reflect on you, but every man is judged for what is in his heart, and your heart is good. I will never forget you, and I will always wonder..." She felt embarrassed, expressing emotions she didn't even understand. "I will always wonder what could have been, if not for the circumstances surrounding all of this—" She stopped and shook her head. "Forgive me. I don't know what I'm saying."

Jude grasped her arms. "It's *because* of those circumstances you mentioned that it's hard to know what we're really feeling about anything. I just know that I adore you, Ingrid. It won't be easy staying out of your life, but it's the right thing to do."

Their eyes held, and she slowly nodded, then turned away. "Go then."

"Ingrid—"

"Go. Just go," she said softly.

She heard a deep sigh. "Thank you for sitting with me after I was shot." There came another sigh. "Ingrid—"

"Go."

She felt his hand on her shoulder, but she refused to look at him.

"I hope you'll come to the meeting," he told her.

"It's at four o'clock at the town hall. I want you to know that I've made up my mind to forgive Gunter Sternaman and have made arrangements to have him released with no charges against him. That should help ease the tensions around here and maybe even help me find that God of yours."

Ingrid nodded. "He is your God, too, Jude, just waiting quietly for you to seek Him out."

He squeezed her shoulder before letting go.

After he went out the door, Ingrid stood there feeling numb. Jude was indeed a different and better man than when he first came to Plum Creek last spring...a lifetime ago. Maybe that was her answer for why God had brought him into her life. If she'd had even a tiny hand in the changes in Jude's heart, had anything to do with him giving more thought to God and forgiveness, maybe that was all God wanted of her.

He was out of her life, and that was best, yet she couldn't help her tears. She decided she would not attend the meeting later; her father could go without her. They'd said their goodbyes and now it was time to forget Jude Kingman ever walked into her life.

Chapter Twenty-One

Early November

"**W**ell, this is quite a change from the farm, ya?" Albert looked around the busy streets of Omaha as Ingrid guided their horse-drawn wagon, stacked high with only the items necessary to get started someplace new. They'd managed to sell their farm tools and all their animals, and neighboring farmers who were not losing their land had bought most of the furniture, as well as Ingrid's prized Concord cooking range. She'd kept the precious family china, her mother's rocker and a few treasured doilies her mother had made.

Those items, along with clothes, cooking pans, household utensils and what food was salvageable, were packed in trunks and boxes in the back of their wagon. They'd set out a week ago for Omaha, camping along the way and traveling by wagon to save money. Making the trip using the very railroad that had put them in this position was too expensive for their limited funds, money that might be needed for something more important.

During the long, cold journey Ingrid could hardly stop thinking about Jude. Her father told her that at the meeting held in Plum Creek, he'd indeed announced, to everyone's shock, that he would not press charges against Gunter Sternaman, and that he had made arrangements for the man's release. Ingrid knew the move was an attempt by Jude to make amends for hurting so many people. He'd even promised financial help for Plum Creek, in the form of a grain elevator the railroad would build there.

Ingrid was proud of Jude for his efforts, especially considering it was likely his father was not at all happy with the decision. Jude seemed to be making an honest attempt to change his life for the better.

She maneuvered the wagon through the streets of Omaha, forcing away her thoughts of Jude, but when they passed a large brick building that bore the sign Kingman Enterprises, her heart skipped a beat. She remembered what Jude said about going there for help if necessary, but she vowed she would not do so. She did not want to risk involvement with Jude again.

She looked away and concentrated on other businesses, taking note of those where she or her father might find work. Johnny kept pointing out various big buildings and exclaiming over the size of the railroad yard and how many people there were milling about and in general what a wonderful place Omaha would be to live. Little did the boy realize what a traumatic change this was for his father and even for Ingrid. Neither of them had known anything but the farm.

They made their way to the east side of town and headed for the residential areas, where a real estate agent had told them they would find a small home to rent.

"You were right that Omaha would be noisy and crowded, Far," she told Albert. "It is certainly nothing like Plum Creek."

"Ya, but ve must make the best of things.

Johnny vill get a better education here, huh? Maybe ve be happier here after all."

"Ya, Far." Happier? Until Ingrid could get rid of the tangle of emotions inside her regarding Jude Kingman, she would never be truly happy. Still, she was glad her father was trying to make the best of things. It was so much harder for an older person to adjust. They had at least received a fair price for their belongings, and Albert's back was feeling better, so they had that much for which to be thankful.

"Maybe you vill find a husband here, ya?" Albert added. "Maybe a banker or something, a nice man who can provide vell for you but is not from an uppity family like those Kingmans."

"Ya," Ingrid again agreed. There was no use trying to explain her feelings to her father. He would never understand. She'd not spoken to Jude again after that day in church. That afternoon they had signed the farmland over to the railroad, but Jude left the paperwork to hired men and had left for Chicago right after his meeting.

Gone. Jude was gone for good this time. Now all Ingrid had to do was find a way to banish him from her thoughts. Her life had turned into an endless swirl of bewilderment, change and readjustment. Maybe her father was right. Maybe here in a new town she would find a fine young man better suited to someone brought up as she was.

After another twenty minutes of bouncing over brick streets they reached the edge of the city and began passing the larger homes closest to town, mostly Victorian structures that likely belonged to Omaha's wealthier citizens. She couldn't help wondering what the Kingman home in Chicago must be like.

After several blocks the brick streets ended and turned to gravel. Ingrid spotted more modest homes to the left and headed in that direction.

"This is too far from town," Johnny complained.

"We have no choice, Johnny," Ingrid told him. "You saw those big homes near the city. We could never afford to live there."

They began passing smaller but tidy homes and saw a For Rent sign in front of a little square log home that looked sturdy and solid and appeared to have a good roof. Big paned windows dressed each side of a central wooden front door, and an overhang supported by wooden posts provided shade for the front porch along the entire length of the house.

"I think this is the one the realtor told us about," Ingrid told her father, steering the horses into the little rutted driveway. She climbed down and walked closer, anxious to find a place to call home.

The front porch had no floor but rather consisted of large, flat stones in the ground.

Ingrid tried the front door after getting no response to a knock, but it was locked. All three of them began peering into the windows and Ingrid saw hardwood floors, a fireplace, a large, square porcelain kitchen sink with a hand pump, a wooden table, two wooden rockers and an iron cookstove nowhere near as nice as her Concord, but it would do. There appeared to be two bedrooms at the back of the main room, and Ingrid saw a stairway.

"There must be another bedroom upstairs," she commented. "This looks fine, don't you think, Far? And it has an indoor water pump. That is something we did not have on the farm."

They walked farther away and studied the outer structure. "Good and solid," Albert commented.

"And it's wood instead of sod," Ingrid added, "with big windows."

They walked around the cabin, peering in back windows to see a rope spring bed in one of the rear bedrooms.

"At least there is a little furniture," Ingrid commented. "And it looks clean." She glanced at a privy in the backyard that looked freshly painted. "I like it just fine."

They walked around to the front again to see a neatly dressed, middle-aged man riding toward them in a one-man carriage. He came up the driveway and halted the carriage near them, greeting them with a smile as he climbed out of the buggy. He wore a well-tailored suit and a small round hat, his shoes shined. "Hello there!" he shouted, peering at them over a pair of small spectacles.

Ingrid and her father greeted him. "Do you know anything about this house?" Ingrid asked.

"I certainly do." He put out his hand. "My name is Jared Sims, and I live two houses away. This house belongs to a man named Matthew Oberhue, and I am in charge of renting it for him."

"I am Ingrid Svensson, and this is my father, Albert, and my brother, Johnny." They all shook hands. "How much is the rent, Mr. Sims?"

"Five dollars a month."

Ingrid looked at Albert. "What do you think?"

"I like it!" Johnny exclaimed.

"There is a school just six blocks north of here," Jared told them, pointing. "You can get the boy enrolled there tomorrow. School has been in session only a couple of weeks because of time off for farmers."

"Ya, ve know about time off for farming," Albert said sadly.

"We'll take the house," Ingrid told Jared. "But we must find jobs soon if we are to keep up the rent."

"Well, I do know they always need help at the railroad yards, what with Omaha growing so fast and more trains coming through. You might check that out, Mr. Svensson." He climbed back into his carriage. "I'll go see Mr. Oberhue about the house. The place isn't very big, but it's been well maintained and has no leaks." He tipped his hat to Ingrid and drove off, promising to come right back.

Ingrid turned to gaze at the humble little house. Johnny was running around looking in the windows again.

"The railroad yards," Albert grumbled. "The railroad steals my farm, and now I might end up vorking for them." He shook his head. "It is not fair that life should be this vay for us, not fair at all."

Ingrid thought of Jude and never seeing him again. "Many things in life are not as they should be, Far. At least we have a home again, and the hope of work, and a good school for Johnny. It is more than we could have hoped for not long ago."

"Ya, I suppose." Albert put a hand to her waist. "You are such a good girl, Ingrid. You take good care of me and Johnny. I know this has all been hard on you, and I know you cared for that Jude

Kingman. But I am glad he is out of our lives now. It is best, ya? You know it is best."

Ingrid pondered his words for a moment. Her father had no idea how much she'd cared for Jude. "I know only that we are here and starting life over, Far. Right now I do not know what is best and what is not. I only know we must make the best of what we have and go on from here, making a good life for Johnny. *Mor* would have wanted that."

She'd not used the Swedish term for mother in years, but right now she dearly wished the woman was with them, wished she could cry on her mother's shoulder. At the moment she felt like a lost little girl.

Chapter Twenty-Two

Late December

A grand display of delightful Christmas decorations dazzled the Kingman mansion. Live greens
hung across the entire front veranda and around all
the fireplaces. Expensive, handblown glass orna-
ments dangled from beautifully decorated Christmas trees that adorned nearly every room. The tree
in the ballroom was fifteen feet high, touching the
ceiling and filling the room with its rich, pine aroma.

Jude wondered how Ingrid was spending her
Christmas. Very simply, he supposed, and with the

joy a true Christian should feel on this holiday. His mother, on the other hand, was simply happy to have a reason to invite every wealthy person in Chicago to the mansion for a grand gala. He watched her float around the room, greeting business associates, judges, lawyers, doctors, politicians and the like, sparkling in diamonds and rubies and a deep green velvet gown.

Mark followed suit. He was his mother's son, meeting and greeting guests and enjoying his importance. Jude could hardly stomach his brother's jovial smile and his eager hand-shaking. The man apparently felt no remorse for what he'd done, but rather he was probably celebrating the fact that he'd gotten away with it. Jude wondered if his father knew, or if he would even care.

"Jude!"

Jude turned to see Catherine Gables, a young woman he'd known since she was just a little girl. When she was old enough, he'd dated her for a short time. The daughter of a city banker and councilman running for the Illinois Senate, Catherine was sophisticated and well educated, and she was not as superficial as most young women he'd known.

"Merry Christmas, Jude!"

Jude brightened. "And Merry Christmas to you.

I haven't seen you for quite some time, Catherine."
He leaned down to kiss her cheek.

"I've missed you, Jude. I'm told you spent a lot of time at the Omaha office this past summer."

He shrugged. "I spent most of the summer in a little farm town called Plum Creek, but my work there is finished now."

She frowned, looking him over. "I certainly hope so! Mother told me you were *shot*! Is it really true, Jude?"

He turned to a passing waiter to take two beverages from the tray, and handed one to Catherine. "A disgruntled farmer decided that he might end all his troubles if he put a bullet in me."

"That's terrible! I had no idea. I was at a finishing school in New York all summer." She stood back and looked him over. "You look all right. Are you all healed?"

He sipped his hot lemon and sugar drink. "I'm fine."

"I'm so glad. I hope the man who shot you was properly punished."

Jude grinned. "Actually, no." He swallowed more of his drink and set the cup on a fireplace mantel. "I forgave him."

Catherine just stared at him a moment, then

burst into laughter. "*Forgave* him? Jude, no King-man alive would forgive a lowly farmer for trying to kill him! What prompted you to do such a thing?"

He thought how pretty Ingrid would look wearing what Catherine wore, a deep blue taffeta dress with a scooped neckline, a diamond necklace decorating her throat, her hair wound and pinned into beautiful curls that danced around diamond earrings. If Ingrid were here right now she'd knock every other young woman over with jealousy. "I guess I got religion," he answered.

Catherine laughed again, taking a sip of her drink. "This is getting more and more bizarre. What on earth happened to you down in Omaha? You forgive a man who shoots you, and you tell me you got religion?"

She sobered as Jude watched her almost sadly, realizing again how shallow most of the women he'd known could be. He'd thought Catherine was different.

She studied him closer. "You're serious, aren't you?" she asked.

Jude breathed deeply. "Could be."

She set her own cup on the mantel. "Then I'm sorry I laughed."

His hopes for a decent woman among his own kind rose again. "Apology accepted."

She grasped his arm and pulled him to the side of the room behind a table resplendent with a Christmas tree-shaped cake and beautiful candelabras. A small symphonic orchestra played a beautiful waltz, and couples floated around the ballroom floor to the music while Catherine took hold of one of Jude's hands.

"We've been friends since I was little and used to kick you in the shins and make you yell at me. I know you, Jude Kingman. Tell me what's *really* going on."

"I'm not sure what you mean."

"Yes, you do. You've changed. Something tells me it was more than getting shot that did it. You've met someone, haven't you, someone who had a profound impact on your life for some reason? Is it a woman?"

He smiled softly. "You are insightful, Catherine."

"I knew it! Tell me!"

"You won't be jealous?"

"Of *course* I'll be jealous. How could I not be? I've had visions of walking down the aisle with you since I was six years old! But I am perfectly aware that you have no such feelings for me, and so I'll tell you my own news. I am engaged!" She pulled off a long white glove and wiggled the fingers of her left hand, causing a large diamond on her ring finger to sparkle.

"Well, congratulations!" he said sincerely. "And who is the lucky fellow?"

"His name is Gabriel Booker. I met him in New York, and it was love at first sight! Gabriel is a lawyer and comes from a wonderful family. Tell me you're happy for me, Jude."

"I'm happy for you."

She batted her eyes at him. "Of course, you could break the engagement by asking me to marry *you* instead."

He laughed lightly. "That is very tempting."

She put on an air of disappointment. "But it won't happen. Is it because of the mysterious person you've met, who, by the way, you still haven't told me about? We got off the subject, Jude Kingman. Who is it that has made you a changed man?"

He shrugged. "I don't know that I'm completely changed. Besides, it's someone I have no business being interested in and who in turn would not have the slightest interest in anything serious with me. It was over before it began."

"What woman would not be interested in the dashingly handsome and rich Jude Kingman?"

He snickered. "One with a lot of common sense

and a realistic vision of who I am and who she is and who knows it would never work—and that's besides the fact that I don't even know if she cares one whit for me."

"Anything can work if love is involved. Do you love her?"

"Actually, I do, but we both know it can never be. She's a Swedish farm girl who was living in a soddy when I met her and has never in her whole life worn a dress like you are wearing right now."

Catherine frowned with curiosity. "Swedish? Then she must have blond hair and blue eyes, and she must be the most beautiful female you've ever met. Nothing but the best would turn the head of Chicago's most notorious womanizer."

He laughed louder. "I have never been a womanizer, Catherine Gables, let alone a notorious one. I have no idea how such a rumor got started."

"Because women fall all over you, that's how, and don't try to tell me you haven't taken advantage of that more than once."

"Well, I've met someone who has shown me that all the others mean nothing."

She pouted. "Including me?"

"You're spoken for, remember?"

She smiled flirtatiously. "I still need to know I mean *something* to you."

"You know you do." He tugged at a dangling curl. "Where is the lucky fellow who's marrying you?"

"He's getting his masters at Harvard and decided to use the holidays to study. He wants to finish early so we can be married next summer."

"Well, be sure to invite me."

"Of course we will. And you may bring your Swedish sweetheart."

"She's not my sweetheart. She's a friend."

"I see. A woman who can actually resist Jude Kingman. Now, that *is* an anomaly." Catherine studied him. "You're truly smitten, aren't you?"

Jude sobered. "I think I am, but there is no future in it, Catherine."

"And who is telling you that?"

He smiled sadly. "*She* is, and my own conscience and common sense. And of course my own family thinks I'm crazy and would probably disown me if I brought a foreign peasant girl into the family. That's the way they put it, anyway. I don't see her that way. Ingrid's a beautiful, strong, brave woman of deep faith."

"Ingrid? I like that name."

"So do I. And believe it or not, it's her good qualities and her deep faith that attracted me more than her physical beauty. She taught me the importance of faith in our lives."

"My!" Catherine stepped back. "This woman *has* changed you! Why are you letting her protests and your family's opinion stop you from pursuing a relationship with her? If she makes you happy, why let *anything* stop you?"

He shrugged. "Surely you can imagine how she'd be treated by my family. I'd never do that to her. She's better off marrying some man in whose world she can feel comfortable."

Catherine folded her arms. "What if *you* tried to fit into *her* world?"

He knit his eyebrows together in surprise. "When did you become so wise?"

"I really don't know. I guess it's just that I want you to be as happy as I am. If you're pining for this woman and think she wouldn't like it here, then adjust to her way of life." She leaned up to kiss his cheek. "You have always been special to me, Jude. I hope you can work this out."

He smiled warmly. "It's not that simple. Believe me, I've thought of going to Omaha to live, but there are some...what you might call...extenuating circumstances." *Like my brother killing Ingrid's closest friend and neighbor.*

Catherine rolled her eyes as she pulled her glove back on. "Take my advice and don't let that woman get away. She's in your blood, I can tell."

"I'll give it serious consideration, oh wise one."

She laughed and grabbed his hand. "Right now I think we should have one last dance before I marry someone else!" She pulled him to the dance floor. Jude put a hand to her waist and they whirled around the room to a waltz.

Jude wondered if Ingrid had ever danced, or even been held lovingly in a man's arms. How he would love teaching her to dance. He missed her so! How in the world was he going to keep his promise to stay out of her life?

Chapter Twenty-Three

December 25, 1873

"'Then Joseph, being raised from sleep, did as the angel of the Lord had bidden him and took unto him his wife: And knew her not till she had brought forth her firstborn son: and he called his name Jesus.'"

"That was very good, Johnny," Ingrid told him.

"Ya, my son can read good," Albert said proudly. "Johnny vill go far in this country, in spite of not having the farm. The only thing that helps the hurt in my heart is knowing how smart my son is and that he vill be just fine vitout the farm, ya?"

Johnny grinned shyly. "I miss the farm sometimes, but I like it here, too."

"Ya, that is good," Albert replied, a lingering
sorrow in his eyes.

They all sat on a braided rug in front of the fireplace and a small pine tree decorated with strung
popcorn. Ingrid reached behind her, picking up two
presents. "Here are your gifts, simple as they are."

Albert smiled. "Ve have alvays kept Christmas
simple, daughter." He took the package and gently
opened the brown paper in which it was wrapped,
then held up a red-and-black flannel shirt.

"I know how cold it gets down at the railroad
yards, Far. Be sure to wear that shirt under your
sweater and jacket."

"It is so nice, Ingrid. How did you make this vitout me knowing about it?"

Ingrid laughed. "It was not easy, especially with
the hours I have put in at Mr. Oberhue's store."

"It is vonderful," Albert exclaimed, "too good
to vear for vork."

Ingrid took pleasure in his joy. "You had *better*
wear it for work! That is why I made it." It felt
good to have decent jobs, although the pay was
nominal. Their bellies were full and they were
warm, which was all that mattered. She was adapt-
ing to working at Oberhue's, a store that sold ma-

terial and all kinds of sewing supplies. Her biggest
worry was her father's job of coupling and uncou-
pling trains at the railroad yards. "You work hard,
Far, and this time of year it's so cold down at the
yards."

He waved her off. "It keeps me busy and brings
home money. That is all that matters." He turned
to Johnny. "Open your present, Johnny!"

The boy tore into the brown wrapping and
pulled out a handsome pocketknife. "Ingrid, I love
it! I can't believe you finally think I'm old enough
for one of these. Thanks!"

Ingrid gave him a chastising look. "You use that
carefully and only for the very most necessary reasons. Remember that it is not a toy."

"I will." He fondled the knife, pulling out the
blade and then putting it back again. "Gosh, Ingrid,
it must have cost a lot. You shouldn't have spent
so much."

"Mr. Oberhue found it for me at a discount. Besides, he likes you very much, Johnny. You are a
big help when you come in on weekends to sweep
up the store for him and help with inventory."

Johnny smiled with pride, turning to his father.
"Can I help you at the railroad yards this weekend
instead, Far? Mr. Oberhue said he won't need me
Sunday, and I like watching the trains."

"It is too dangerous," Albert replied with a frown.

"I'd be careful. I like to watch the big steam engines. I'll do whatever you tell me. Don't forget that I'm eleven now. And I've grown about five inches since last spring. I'm almost a man!"

"How well I know that!" Ingrid added. "I am the one who makes your pants."

Albert sighed. "I vill ask my boss," he told Johnny. "You can probably help out, but you must mind everything I tell you." He brightened then, reaching for a package that he handed to Ingrid. "Here you are, daughter, from me and Johnny together."

"Oh, Far!" She looked from Albert to Johnny. "Thank you so much. Johnny, you are supposed to use what little you are able to save for higher schooling."

"I know, but you do so much for us, Ingrid."

She smiled humbly and carefully removed brown paper from a box inside which lay a lovely comb, brush and mirror set. Ingrid gasped. "It's beautiful!"

"Far put in more money than I did, but we knew you'd like it," Johnny told her excitedly.

"It is for your beautiful, beautiful hair," Albert told her. "I just vish, daughter, that you vould find a good man now who could take care of you and let you be home to raise children. Here in this big town, I'll bet you have had more than von young man pay you some attention."

Ingrid felt herself blushing. "There have been a few." *But no one who could hold a candle to Jude Kingman,* she thought. She looked down at the brush set, studying the lovely filigree work around the silver handles. She could not help wondering what the holiday must be like for the Kingmans. Jude's mother probably threw wonderful Christmas parties, and she could only guess at the kind of presents people like that gave each other.

How did Jude feel about Christmas? Did he and his family recognize it as the birth of their Lord and Savior, or simply as a time to have parties and spend money? Did Jude have a special someone to whom he'd given a gift today?

"Ingrid?"

She looked up from the brush set. "Yes?"

"Did you not hear a vord I just said?" Albert asked.

She blushed. "Oh, I am sorry! I was just thinking how beautiful this brush set is."

"Vell, I vas asking about one man in particular. Has not that young livery owner, Daniel Piner, been paying you many visits? He came and talked to me, you know."

She sighed and got to her feet. "I have no interest in him, Far, and you must stop picking my beaus for me," she told him with a protesting tone. "I will find love all in good time, but it will be someone I want to see, not someone you *think* I should." She set the brush set on a side table. "No more talk about men. Let's enjoy a nice dinner and be happy that we have each other. Even if I was interested in someone else, you and Johnny still need me to take care of you. Whoever wants me for a wife will have to accept my father and my brother along with me, and not every man will do that."

Her father stood up, and she gave him a hug. "Thank you for the gift, Far." She turned to Johnny. "And you, too, Johnny." She embraced her brother.

"Thank you for the knife."

"And for the shirt," Albert told her.

Smiling, Ingrid took their hands. "Come and sit. I have a wonderful meal ready!"

She hurried to the range to check the food, thinking what a nice Christmas it had turned out to be in spite of the disappointments of the past summer and fall. They enjoyed their little house, and though their tree was rather deficient in shape and size and decorations, she thought it beautiful.

Albert seemed to be feeling less dejected about losing the farm, and Johnny was doing well in school. She worked long hours at Oberhue's, but long hours meant more money, and she was determined to put some aside for Johnny's education. She wondered if her father truly understood that between working and taking care of him and Johnny and their home, there was hardly time for seeing prospective husbands. Little had changed in that part of her life.

She stirred the gravy, still disturbed by lingering thoughts of Jude. Since meeting and getting to know him, she seemed unable to take any interest in anyone else. Perhaps she was not meant to marry at all.

Merry Christmas, Jude. May God help you find happiness.

Chapter Twenty-Four

Late January, 1874

Jude stared out the window at the busy street below, thinking how early it got dark this time of year. The takeover of farmland by the railroad had caused him a great deal of legal paperwork that kept him at the office well after closing time. That, at least, was an excuse not to be in a hurry to go home.

He noticed Christmas decorations still hung in some store windows. Horses pulling all sizes and styles of wagons and carriages splattered up and down the dimly lit street below, wet from a new-fallen snow. January had a way of feeling extra cold in the city, it seemed. Everything got cold—concrete, bricks, steel. He touched the window of his third-floor office. Cold. Cold as he was cold inside, but not from the weather.

He watched drifting snowflakes, wondering if snow was falling in Omaha, if Ingrid was walking through it to get to and from work. Maybe she rode a horse to work. She certainly could not afford a taxi carriage, and it would be a lot of work to hitch a wagon every day just to go into town.

He knew where she worked and where Albert worked. Much as he realized he needed to forget about her, he'd had Wilson find out where she lived and if she was all right. He hated the thought of her being cold and alone, shivering against a winter wind and snow stinging her face just to go to work every day so the family could make ends meet. She was far too special to live like that. She should be in her own lovely home baking her delicious bread and tending to children. What a wonderful mother she would make, nothing like his own cold, unfeeling mother who'd never shown him one ounce of affection. He could envision Ingrid holding a sweet baby, rocking him, singing to him. He wondered how it felt to be held and loved by a mother.

He shook his head and turned away, returning to his desk. Never had he felt so alone and out of place. Ever since last summer, seeing the heartache of those farmers, feeling responsible for the loss of so many dreams, realizing his own brother was so evil and loving a woman he could never have—ever since all of that he'd never felt so alone in the world.

Before going to Plum Creek, he'd already felt lonely, but not like this. He felt an unprecedented emptiness since knowing Ingrid, the one person out there to whom he could open his heart and who would listen without making fun of one word he said. She seemed to understand his every feeling, and she cared enough to pray for him. No one in the family had ever offered such a thing, and in fact, he doubted any of them even knew how to pray. Superficially, yes. But with belief and sincerity—no.

He sat down at his desk, staring at a ledger that he didn't really care about. What he wanted to do was talk to Ingrid. He wanted to touch her, smell her, kiss her, look into her big blue eyes again, admire her glowing blond tresses, gaze upon her beautiful smile. But to see her again would be disaster. They'd been right in their decision to never again see each other. The pain of being together and discovering what a mistake they'd made would be much worse than the pain of ending everything before it could even begin. Surely they had chosen wisely.

Heavy. That was how he felt. Heavy with a need for Ingrid Svensson. Heavy with loneliness. Heavy with a feeling of being unwanted by his own family, for reasons he could not even name. He had a good life, stood to inherit a fortune one day, already had a fortune at his hands to spend however he chose. Why didn't that make him happy? Ingrid would know the answer. She led such a simple life, never knowing from one year to the next if there would be enough money for food, yet she was such a solid, confident woman, so full of trust that life would be just fine as long as God was in it.

The heaviness he felt was made worse by the knowledge of Mark's deed. He felt the weight of the guilt that he knew but was unable to do anything about. *God knows,* Ingrid had told him. *God will see he is punished, either in this life or the next.*

Maybe she was right. It wasn't his place to judge or defend, and with no proof, not even the proper authorities could do that. And so here he was, stuck in one track that went nowhere, like sidetracks along the railroad that led only so far and then ended.

He had to do something to get out of this depression. He couldn't live out his life this way. Maybe he should force himself to start seeing other women, decent women who might make a good wife and mother, if such women could be found among his family's circle of friends. He might have to go outside that circle, but he had to do something to get his life back. Maybe a wife and family would help him see his purpose in life, and help him forget about Ingrid.

Maybe he should pray about it. That's what Ingrid would tell him to do. He'd tried praying several times but wasn't so sure he was doing it right, or that the Good Lord listened to people like him. He wondered if Ingrid was praying for the same thing he was: to find someone to love. Maybe she was asking God to help her forget about Jude Kingman. He smiled wryly at the thought of it.

He got up again and went to the coat stand, taking down his expensive black wool coat and pulling it on, then placing a black felt hat on his head. He turned off the ceiling light, thinking how he was growing used to the wonderful invention of electricity. Ingrid still worked at home by the light of oil lamps.

He walked out and along the hall, down three flights of stairs and out into the street. After hailing a cab, he climbed into the carriage and ordered the driver to take him to the nearest church or cathedral. He would go there and pray. Just the thought of it lifted his spirits. He would again ask God to guide him in what he should do about his family, to help him with his concern over what Mark had done—and most of all to bring him an answer as to what he should do about the fire that came into his blood and heart every time he thought about Ingrid Svensson. Ingrid claimed God had an answer for everything. He was still waiting for some of those answers.

Chapter Twenty-Five

Mid-February

"I think this is the best color for you, Mrs. Winters," Ingrid told one of her customers. "The soft green in it brings out the green in your eyes."

Lilly Winters beamed. "You are so sweet, Ingrid, and always such a help." She turned to Matt Oberhue. "You did right hiring this wonderful young woman, Mr. Oberhue. I'm so afraid some man will come along and whisk her away in marriage and she won't be working here any longer."

Oberhue nodded. "I'm worried about the same

thing. Plenty of men, young and old, have taken a second look, that's for sure." He turned to Ingrid with a scolding look. "Ingrid keeps turning down their requests for dinner or dances, even church socials."

Ingrid blushed. "Mr. Oberhue, I am just not interested. All of you people must stop trying to marry me off. A woman does not need to marry to be happy."

Mrs. Winters gasped. "Ingrid! Such talk! A beautiful young woman like you should most certainly be married. What a wonderful wife and mother you would make."

The thought brought a longing to Ingrid's heart, but she still could not imagine taking any of the men in town for a husband.

The passing of time had helped lessen her thoughts of Jude, but it could not erase the lingering jumble of feelings. By now she guessed Jude had put her memory behind him and perhaps was seeing someone. She'd heard nothing from him for months, and that was good. He was sticking to their decision to stay in their own separate worlds.

Maybe she *should* answer the requests from some of the available men who came into the store and invited her to social events. Was she a fool to keep putting them off, to turn down a chance at love and family?

She began measuring the material Mrs. Winters had just ordered. Then the door suddenly burst open. A young man wearing a heavy, soiled work coat and a railroad cap ran up to Ingrid's counter.

"Miss Svensson!"

Ingrid lost her smile, recognizing Hugh Kerry, a man who worked with her father in the railroad yards.

"What is it, Hugh?"

"You'd best come quick! Fact is, you'd best go over to the hospital and wait there!"

Ingrid felt her heart plummet toward her stomach. "Hugh, what's happened?"

True sorrow filled his brown eyes as he removed his hat. "Ma'am, I'm afraid your father—he's been killed. And your brother is hurt real bad."

Now it seemed the blood was draining from her body. "What!"

"Lord, help us!" Oberhue exclaimed.

"Oh, Ingrid, how awful!" Mrs. Winters told her.

Ingrid put down her measuring tape and hurried toward the back of the store to get her wool, hooded cape.

"It was an accident, ma'am," Hugh called to her. "Your pa was showing Johnny how to link the couples. Johnny started to fall as the two cars were heading for each other and your pa grabbed for him. They both fell then, and your pa got caught between the couplings."

Ingrid felt her world coming apart again as she returned from the back room.

"It was too late to stop it," he continued, both horror and sorrow in his eyes. "The couplings came together right at your pa's chest."

Ingrid felt faint.

"If it's any consolation, ma'am, he died instantly," Hugh explained, "but Johnny, he hit his head really bad. He's unconscious. He might already be at the hospital. I mean, they rushed him off real fast."

Ingrid struggled to stay calm. "Will you help me rehitch my horse and carriage? I keep my horse on a tether in back."

"I brought a wagon from the railroad. It's not as comfortable, but—"

"Fine!" Ingrid rushed for the door. "Let's hurry!"

"We'll pray for Johnny, Ingrid!" Oberhue shouted after her.

Everything seemed to swirl around Ingrid in a blur of unreality. She climbed blindly into the wagon, hardly aware that Hugh climbed in after her. She clung to the seat frame as he slapped the reins and got the horse pulling the wagon at as fast a trot as he dared on such a busy street.

Ingrid did not notice people or carriages or

buildings or even how cold it was as they hurried on for several blocks toward Omaha's one and only hospital. Would the doctors there know what to do with Johnny? Could they save him? Would he regain consciousness? And what had been done with her father's body?

Far! He'd just begun to adjust to living here, his heart just beginning to heal from losing the farm. Now this! She never had a chance to say goodbye!

"I'm so sorry, Miss Svensson. It wasn't anything anyone could have stopped."

She hadn't wanted Johnny to go help their father this weekend, but the boy was so excited about going. *I'm eleven. I'm old enough to help out more, and I'm caught up on my schoolwork. Please, Ingrid? Please can I go to the railroad yard?*

Such a good boy he was. He'd never complained about the hard work on the farm. He'd never complained when they lost it and he had to come here and make new friends. He never complained about working after school to make a little extra money to help out. And he had so much promise for a wonderful future.

What if he died? What if she lost *both* of them? She would have no one. In less than one year everything important to her would have slipped away.

You still have Me.

She could feel God speaking the words.

Lord, I do not know if I am strong enough this time. Please help me! What shall I do? How can I bear this? Please, please, do not take Johnny from me, too!

They arrived at the hospital. Hugh helped her down from the wagon. She clung to his arm as he led her up the steps and inside, worried she'd collapse if she let go. Hugh asked where Johnny was, then helped rush her to a room where doctors were looking into the boy's lifeless eyes.

"Johnny!" Ingrid rushed to his side. "How bad is he? I am his only living relative—his sister, Ingrid Svensson."

A faceless doctor looked at her, his voice sounding far away. "I'm afraid his brain might be swelling. If it gets too bad, Mrs. Svensson—"

"It's *Miss* Svensson," she interrupted. What a silly thing to say. Who cared?

"He could die, ma'am, if the swelling doesn't go down in another twenty-four hours."

She stared at Johnny. His skin looked pasty and gray. He already appeared dead. "I—isn't there— can't you do something to help him?"

The doctor sighed. "Only a specialist can do that. I know of one in Chicago, but it would be a very expensive operation."

I am with you. There were those words again.

Help me! She looked at the doctor again. She didn't even know his name. "The train. He could get to Chicago quickly by train, couldn't he?" She turned to Hugh. "Surely since this was a railroad accident, the railroad will pay to transfer him to a hospital in Chicago!"

"I expect so, ma'am, but then again, he wasn't actually a railroad employee."

"We must take him to Chicago!" Ingrid looked back at the doctor. "Please write a quick letter to the doctor of whom you speak. Give it to me and I will have Johnny taken there!"

"Ma'am, the cost—"

"It does not matter! If the railroad will not help, I will work to my dying day to pay for it. I cannot bear losing my last living relative! Surely this doctor you speak of has enough compassion to take the financial risk."

The doctor sighed. "Yes, ma'am."

He hurried away, and Ingrid took hold of Johnny's hand, kissing it before closing her eyes to pray. "Dear God in Heaven, please save this innocent boy. And please give me the strength I need."

She sat down on the edge of the bed and let the tears come. Her beloved Far was gone from her life, and Johnny might be dying. "Oh, God, bring me help," she begged. "Don't take Johnny from me. He is so young. Please save him!"

She thought of Christ's words on the cross: *My God, My God, why hast Thou forsaken me?*

Chapter Twenty-Six

Ingrid sat watching Johnny, not quite a man yet, so much of his life ahead of him. Only an operation might save him. Otherwise, according to Dr. Henry Roush here at the Sisters of Mercy Hospital in Chicago—the only surgeon in all of Illinois, Missouri and Nebraska who could perform the dangerous procedure—Johnny would die within twenty-four to forty-eight hours.

Yesterday two doctors arrived in Omaha to accompany Johnny on the trip by train to Chicago. They told Ingrid that the railroad had set up the operation, but she had no idea if that meant they would give her any financial help. Considering how they had already nearly destroyed her life, she had little hope of any assistance now.

Nurses doted over Johnny, keeping constant watch until preparations for the surgery were finished. Dr. Roush had arrived only an hour ago.

She felt so alone sitting here in a big hospital in a city so large and noisy and busy that it practically frightened her, surrounded by strangers, and putting her precious little brother's life into the hands of a doctor she'd met only sixty minutes ago. She prayed constantly for Johnny, and she so longed to have someone to lean on. It should be Far, but Far was gone. She had no one. No one. Even God seemed far away.

"Far," she wept, feeling lost. She didn't even realize that someone had walked into the room until a hand touched her shoulder.

"Ingrid."

Ingrid wiped her eyes and looked up at the man who stood there.

"Jude!" she cried out. She could not help herself. She stood up and threw her arms around him, bursting into tears of relief. The wonderful comfort of strong arms came around her, pressing her close, holding her so tightly.

"It's all right."

She burst forth in a garbled mess of "He's dying! Far is dead! I can't take any more losses! If I lose Johnny I have no one!"

"That's not true. You have me."

Had he really said that?

"I can't believe you didn't have someone get hold of me about this," Jude told her. "I told you once that you could always come to me for help. When I heard about this, I made immediate arrangements to get Johnny up here for the proper surgery."

"Oh, don't let go of me!" Ingrid wept, unable to control her emotions.

"I most certainly will not let go of you," Jude answered. "I don't intend to *ever* let go of you again."

"I thought I was all alone. I hate this big city and so many strangers and—"

"You are not alone, Ingrid. You have your faith, and you have me. I promise you that you will never be alone again if that's what you want. And don't worry about this big city. As soon as Johnny is recovered—and he *will* get through this and recover—I'll get you out of here and back to the peace and quiet of Nebraska." Jude pulled away slightly, refusing to let go of her completely. He took a handkerchief from an inside pocket of his jacket and gently wiped at her tears. "In a small way, this is the answer to my prayers," he told Ingrid. "God found a way to create some good from this tragedy." His dark eyes showed total sincerity. "I love you, Ingrid Svensson. And I want us to be together."

Ingrid took the handkerchief and wiped her nose, resting her head on his shoulder as he again pressed her close. His strong arms felt wonderful...yet how could she think about love at a time like this? "Jude, I've missed you. I am just so sorry it took Far's death to bring us together, and I am so afraid for Johnny. He is such a good boy."

"Johnny will be fine. Dr. Roush is the best, I assure you. And don't worry about the cost for any of this. Whether you like it or not I am paying for everything, and I've already made arrangements for your father's body and his funeral. He's already been buried in a very pleasant area of the cemetery in Omaha. When Johnny is better we'll all go there and have a memorial service over his grave. I also ordered a very nice marker for him."

"Jude, I did not ask for any of those things."

"And that's what I love about you. The only payment I want is for you to marry me, Ingrid. That's worth every last dime I'm worth, and if I had to give it all up for you, then I would. I never should have let my situation get in the way of my love for you."

Everything was spoken with his arms still around her. Ingrid struggled to stop crying so she could comprehend all that was happening. Jude was kissing her hair, her forehead, her eyes, helping her out of the way while nurses came in to move Johnny onto a gurney and wheel him to the operating room.

"Jude, if Johnny dies—"

He grasped her arms and held her away from him then. "What has happened to my strong Ingrid and her undying faith?"

"I—it's just that I've lost so much, Jude. God has to understand I am only human."

He smiled with sympathy. "Of course you are." He led her to a wooden bench in the hallway just outside Johnny's room and made her sit down. Ingrid wiped her eyes and blew her nose again, breathing deeply to get control of herself. "I must look awful," she commented.

"That's impossible."

She faced him then, studying the handsome man beside her, wondering if she was dreaming. "I cannot believe you are really here. I felt so lost and alone."

"And I should be angry with you for not having someone get in touch with me right away. I found out about the accident through a wire from my man in Omaha." He put an arm around her and let her rest her head on his shoulder. "And I'm tired of worrying and wondering about you. I tried to stay way, Ingrid, but I can't. I want us to get married, and if you don't want to live my way, that's fine. We'll build a modest house in Omaha and we'll attend whatever little church suits you and we'll make friends with good Christian people who also live modestly, and we'll have babies and go to church socials and live happily ever after. Just setting eyes on you again tells me I can't walk out of your life a second time. I hope you feel the same way, because if you make me leave, I'll be the most miserable man who ever walked the face of the earth."

Marriage to a man like Jude Kingman? What about their determination that it could never work?

"Just—let me think, Jude. Right now all I can think about is Johnny. He is more like my son than my brother. I have raised him from a baby."

"Then let's just sit here and pray for him. Let me hold you. It feels good. And I'm actually glad you have discovered you are not the strongest human being on earth. We all need holding sometimes, and it's your turn. When was the last time you were able to lean on someone else?"

She took solace in his strong embrace. It felt natural and right. "I can't remember. I am not sure I have *ever* leaned on someone else."

He gently massaged her neck. "Then maybe it's time you learned to let go of that stubborn pride and that determination to be the strong one and let someone else be strong for you. In fact, why don't you lie down on that extra bed in Johnny's room and close your eyes for a while before you collapse? I'll bet you haven't slept since this happened."

"Oh, I couldn't—"

"Yes, you could." He rose and picked her up in strong arms.

"Jude!"

He carried her to the empty hospital bed and laid her on it. "When you're rested we'll go get something to eat," he said with an authoritative air. "Johnny's surgery will take a while."

"Oh, I couldn't leave."

"Then I'll bring you something." He drew a blanket over her shoulders. "And right now you need a little sleep. Give it a try."

"I'll be all right." She started to sit up. He pushed her back down.

"No, you won't. I don't want anything to happen to you, too. Besides, don't forget that Johnny will need us when he gets through this. He doesn't want you collapsing when he needs you most."

Johnny will need us, he'd said. Not "Johnny will need you." He talked as though from here on it would always be "us."

He was serious! It was just beginning to sink in, the reality of it. Jude was here. He'd told her he loved her and wanted to *marry* her! It all began spinning around in her mind in a mixture of terrible sorrow over her father, worry over Johnny, uncertainty about the possibility of a marriage between a wealthy, powerful American businessman and a poor Swedish immigrant who knew nothing about the world he lived in.

Last but not least in the mixture was the growing feeling that now that he'd walked back into her life, she might never be able to let him go again.

He pulled a chair beside the bed and took hold of her hand.

"Jude—"

"Stop talking and sleep," he ordered.

"Will you be here when I wake up?"

"Of course I will. If I had my way we'd get married today and I'd be there every time you woke up for the rest of your life."

She felt a rush of bashfulness and shook her head to clear it of all its conflicting thoughts and emotions. "For now all I can think about is my little brother."

"Of course." Jude turned to a nurse who came in to change the sheets on Johnny's bed. "Can you get this woman something to help her sleep? She's going to need her strength."

"Certainly, Mr. Kingman. I'll check with a doctor."

Mr. Kingman. Ingrid had a suspicion everyone in this hospital knew who Jude was. Probably most of Chicago knew. How strange that a man such as he was in love with her. "Don't go away, Jude," she repeated.

"I told you I wouldn't. When you wake up I'll be right here. I couldn't leave you now. I've dreamed about you every night for far too long to do that."

Ingrid pulled a blanket over her face. "Do not talk that way."

She heard Jude laugh lightly, and she realized he was doing what he could to keep her mind off Johnny. The nurse returned with a pill and a glass of water. "Have her take this, Mr. Kingman. It should help."

"Thank you, dear lady."

Ingrid pulled the blanket away and Jude handed her the water and the pill.

"Swallow this. That's an order. I don't want you

having a nervous breakdown or getting sick just when I've found you again."

Ingrid sat up and swallowed the pill. She lay back down and grasped his hand again. "If you are not here when I wake up, I will never forgive you."

Jude chuckled. He stood up and leaned closer, kissing her cheek…her lips. What a sweet, gentle kiss it was. It was all she remembered before slipping into a deep sleep.

Chapter Twenty-Seven

Ingrid awoke to see Jude still sitting right beside her, just as he'd promised. She sat bolt upright when the realization of where she was hit her. "Johnny!"

Jude pushed her back down. "He's fine. He's in recovery."

Ingrid put a hand to her disheveled hair. "What? You mean I *slept* through it all?" She gasped, sitting up again. "This is terrible!"

"It was the best thing for you. You were completely exhausted, Ingrid."

She put her hands to her face, her thoughts a jumble of mortification at sleeping through

Johnny's surgery and amazement that Jude was still here and—was she remembering right, or had she dreamed the whole thing?—confusion about the things Jude had told her. "I have to see Johnny."

"They won't let you, Ingrid. The doctor drained the fluid from Johnny's brain. He said he came through just fine and that his youth and health are a big plus to his recovery. It's still touch and go, but Dr. Roush doesn't expect any major complications. Why don't we go to the hospital chapel and pray for him? That's the best thing you can do right now for Johnny."

She swung her feet over the edge of the bed, studying Jude's dark eyes. "Are you sure? You are not telling me he will be fine just to make me feel better, are you?"

"No, I am not."

She closed her eyes, feeling weak and completely out of touch with reality. The despair of remembering her father was dead overwhelmed her again, and her chest ached fiercely from grief.

"I'm sure the hospital chapel is a more quiet and soothing place to talk than here. Do you want to go there with me?"

"Yes, we should go there and pray." She felt some loose pins in her hair. "Oh, Jude, what a mess I must be."

He placed his hands at her waist and lifted her down from the bed. "If I had a dollar for every time you've said that to me, I'd be twice as rich as I am now. Quit worrying about such things, Ingrid. I've told you a hundred times over, you always look beautiful to me, whether you're dressed for church or coming out of the fields with kerosene on your hands."

He put an arm around her waist to support her. Feeling perplexed by the day's events, Ingrid let him guide her to the tiny hospital chapel, a small room with just five rows of pews and both a crucifix and a plain cross sitting on an altar at the head of the little room. Jude ushered her into one of the pews and moved in beside her. He put an arm around her again, and feeling terribly weary, Ingrid again rested her head on his shoulder, drinking in the wonderful comfort of his arms.

Jude took hold of the hand in her lap. "Now, we are going to pray, Ingrid, for Johnny and for us. But I need your help. Praying is one thing I'm not very good at."

She squeezed his hand. "God is with us right now, Jude," she said softly, suddenly feeling calmer. "I hope you feel Him, too."

"For the first time in my life, yes, I do."

"Heavenly Father," she prayed, "we beg your

mercy and miracles for Johnny Svensson, a good
boy who believes in You and trusts You to make
him well. We ask that You heal him to total health
and quickly, and that he not suffer too much pain
as he recovers, if this be Your will, Lord Jesus. We
thank you with all our being that Johnny made it
through his surgery, and Lord, I thank you for...for
this man beside me who has chosen out of the
kindness of his heart to pay for Dr. Roush's services, and I thank you that there are men like the
good doctor whose skill and intelligence come
only through Your grace. Surely you sent him to
this world to help those in need and to help You
heal and perform miracles through his hands.

"Last, Lord Jesus, we pray for Albert Harold
Svensson..." She stopped for moment when a lump
came into her throat, and Jude's grip around her
shoulders tightened. "He was—such a good, Christian man, who always served You well. Take him
home, Lord Jesus, and give him green fields to work
with his hands, fine soil where he can make things
grow, a home where he will know only peace and
no pain or heartache. We give him over to you, Lord
Jesus, trusting that he is happy now, perhaps visiting with—" again she felt anguish and a need to
weep. She took a deep breath "—visiting with Carl
and his papa, and with Mama."

Jude sighed and kissed her hair.

"And, Lord Jesus, help Jude understand that the deaths of Carl and his papa are not his fault. His own heart is good, and he must understand that the final judgment comes from You, Lord Jesus. Help Jude understand your grace and mercy, and to find peace in his heart, and help both of us know Your will for us and to find a way to overcome all the things that might come between us.

"Give Papa my love, Lord, and hold my Johnny gently in Your arms so that he knows only peace and no pain as he heals. In the name of our Lord and Savior, Jesus Christ, Amen."

They sat there quietly then in each other's arms for several minutes.

"I've never truly prayed with real belief and earnestness in my whole life," Jude said. "Oh, I've been practicing, but it didn't feel like this. It actually feels kind of good."

Ingrid turned her head upward to look at him. Their eyes held, and in the next moment his lips met hers in a warm kiss that felt good and sweet and right. It was a pure, earnest kiss that told her his love was real, a gentle kiss. He moved his lips to her neck.

"I have everything a man could want in life, Ingrid, and none of it means a thing without you."

He kissed her neck, her cheek, her lips again. "Don't ever again tell me our differences can possibly get in the way of us marrying, because I won't take no for an answer this time. Tell me straight out that you love me and that you will *marry* me."

They kissed again. Ingrid knew that the rush of feelings inside her could no longer be denied but she still had her doubts that they could make it work. "I do love you, Jude," she told him softly, "and I wish I could marry you. But we *do* have to be realistic about our differences. If we marry, I will not live in the manner in which you live here, Jude. I want a simpler life, and I never want people thinking I married you for any reason other than the fact that I love you dearly, for richer or poorer, just as the vows state." Despite her reservations, Ingrid reveled in the fact that she could openly acknowledge and express her feelings for Jude.

"That's fine with me. I told you I'm ready to move to Omaha and build a modest home for us and for Johnny. I already have offices there. It won't be that great a change for me."

Suddenly the memory of his brother's arrogant, mean eyes brought her back to reality. "But it *will* be a great disappointment to your family, Jude. What if you lose your share of Kingman Enterprises? *They* will think I am marrying you for your money, and so they might take it all away from you."

He put a hand to the side of her face. "Ingrid, I have a law degree, and I have plenty of holdings in my own name. I'll open my own practice in Omaha and we will be just fine." He gently caressed her cheek with his fingers. "Please tell me that after the memorial service for your father, and once Johnny is well enough to be at a formal wedding, we will get married."

"I can't say when I'll be ready to marry you just yet, but I can tell you there's nothing I want more."

"Then that will have to be enough for now."

They sat there a while longer, enjoying one another's closeness, reveling in awakening love and both grateful to God for bringing them together. Finally Jude pulled away and helped her up. "Let's go see if we can get in to see Johnny. Once we're sure he's definitely on a road to recovery, I'll go home for a few days and let everyone know I'm marrying you no matter what, Ingrid. Whatever happens, happens. It makes no difference to me anymore, but I promise no one in my family will ever hurt you. *I* will never hurt you. And I'll come back to accompany you to Omaha with Johnny once he's released from here. He'll travel in my personal Pullman where he'll be most comfortable, and I'll arrange for a private nurse for him."

"Jude, you are doing too much."

"Not when it's for the woman I love. I'll have to go back to Chicago once more, this time to clean out my offices and close out certain business dealings and prepare to make my home in Omaha. All I want you to do in the meantime is rest—and think about how much you want to marry me when the time is right."

She smiled, embracing him again. "Yes, when the time is right. And, just so you know, there is only one thing I want from you, Jude, as a wedding present."

"What is that?"

"A new Concord range, the latest and most convenient style."

Jude laughed and shook his head. "I think I can afford that. My, but you're going to be easy to please."

He put an arm around her waist again and led her out of the little chapel. After several minutes of questions and arrangements, they were finally able to see Johnny. All of Ingrid's joy—over her love for Jude and the knowledge that she would one day be his wife—left her at the sight of Johnny's heavily bandaged head and grotesquely swollen face. She nearly collapsed, but Jude's strong arms came around her again.

Everything would be all right. Jude was here.

Chapter Twenty-Eight

Ingrid leaned back in the chair beside Johnny's bed, where she'd sat vigilantly for the past three days. She closed her eyes and thanked God that her brother was making what the doctor termed "a remarkable recovery." Johnny's memory had not been affected, and all his motor skills seemed to be normal.

Poor Johnny. He'd cried and cried over feeling responsible for their father's death. "If I hadn't been clumsy and started to fall…" he said.

She reached over and squeezed Johnny's hand. Through prayer he was learning that he should not feel guilty about what happened. God had chosen to take Albert Svensson, and maybe that was best. Although he'd pretended to adjust to life in Omaha, their father had never been truly happy since losing the farm.

"Now he is happy farming in Heaven," she'd told Johnny, who stirred at that moment and opened his eyes.

"Ingrid?"

Ingrid rose from the chair and leaned closer. "What is it, Johnny?"

"When can we go home?"

"The doctor says in a week or so. And as soon as you are stronger, we will go to Far's grave and have a memorial service for him. And we will get you caught up on your schoolwork."

"Maybe I should quit school and find work. With Far gone, we will need the money."

"Nonsense! I will not allow you to sacrifice your education. Besides, with Far...gone..." Her voice caught. "We will need less food and clothing. I can support both of us."

She wasn't sure what to tell him about Jude. Marriage would mean big changes for all of them. She wanted to wait until Johnny was a bit stronger and until Jude returned, so they could talk to Johnny together about their love and their eventual marriage plans. It would be difficult for Johnny to understand, after thinking of Jude Kingman as the enemy all this time.

Jude had gone home to take care of personal business and to let his family know of his intentions. He would come back to accompany her and Johnny to Omaha. Ingrid still worried about the reaction of Jude's family to his decision. The all-powerful Kingmans would most certainly try their best to change Jude's mind. Was his love for her strong enough to stand up to them? They were going to be furious with him, and she was not going to tell Johnny a thing until Jude returned and she was sure—very, very sure—that she and Jude would indeed marry someday.

"What about all the hospital expenses?" Johnny asked. "How are we going to pay for all of this? I'm so sorry, Ingrid. I've made a mess of things."

She held his hand tightly. "Johnny, it was an accident on railroad property. They are paying for everything, even Far's burial."

Johnny frowned. "This is all that Mr. Kingman's fault and the railroad's fault anyway. If we hadn't lost the farm and had to come here—"

"No, Johnny. There will be no blaming. You are not to blame for Far's death, and neither is the railroad. And Mr. Kingman is a better man than most people realize. He arranged for your surgery, and he promised us a fine, luxurious train car for your trip back to Omaha. He is even going to come with us to help. Right now he is away on business, but he will be back before we leave."

There, she had broken the ice.

"Mr. Kingman did that?"

"Yes. He was only doing his job when he first came to Plum Creek. But he has changed, Johnny, and everyone deserves forgiveness."

A nurse came into the room, interrupting their conversation. "Miss Svensson, a Mrs. Kingman is here to see you. She said she'd like to talk to you alone. She's waiting in an empty office. I can take you there."

Ingrid felt instant alarm. Mrs. Kingman? Jude's *mother*? From the little she knew about the woman from Jude, she suspected the reason for the woman's visit. Feeling suddenly warm and nervous, she took a deep breath, telling herself she must not let the woman intimidate her, if indeed that was the reason for her visit.

She leaned down and kissed Johnny's forehead. "I will be right back, Johnny," she assured him, glad now that Jude had bought her a couple of simple day dresses and other necessities so that she could change clothes while staying with Johnny.

Today she wore a light blue heavy cotton lace dress with a slightly darker blue silk lining that showed through the holes of the lace, a beautiful afternoon dress with three-quarter length sleeves gathered into graceful puffs at the shoulders and fitted at the waist. It was certainly much prettier than anything she'd ever worn, but she'd warned Jude that she was not about to let herself get involved in wearing the best of everything, even when she became Mrs. Jude Kingman, but it did feel good to wear something so lovely.

She smiled now at the memory of how Jude had laughed at a remark she'd made about being "practical and frugal." True to her determination, though, she did not wear long gloves or a fancy hat that matched the colors of the dress, and on her feet she wore the same worn, black high-top shoes with just a slight heel that she'd worn for the past year. They were broken in and comfortable, and besides, they were mostly covered by the flowing lace skirt.

She put a hand to her hair, checking that it was still wound tightly into a bun at the nape of her neck. She wore no jewelry or makeup.

She took a deep breath and followed the nurse down the hallway, steeling her heart against what might be waiting for her. What happened in Chicago? Where was Jude? Did he know about this visit?

She held her head high and kept her shoulders straight as she walked into a small, plain office that contained a wooden desk, chairs, a shelf full of medical books and a stethoscope hanging on the wall.

The nurse closed the door, and a woman who'd been standing at the window turned. Her graying hair was topped with a rose-colored, wide-brimmed hat cocked at the side of her head and decorated with puffs of white lace and white plumes. Her princess-cut visiting suit was made of rose-colored wool, obviously expensive and tailor-made. She wore white gloves on her hands, and a luxurious fur cape hung over the back of one chair, while a matching fur muff sat on the desk.

For a moment the two women just looked at each other, and Ingrid thought how much prettier this woman would look if she showed a hint of joy and a smile instead of the stern, dark look she had on her beautifully made-up face right now.

"Miss Svensson," she said, with a distinct air of dislike.

Ingrid nodded. "You are Mrs. Kingman, Jude's mother." It was so easy now to understand Jude's remarks about his mother. How could anyone feel any love at all from this stiff, cold woman who, at the moment, held a look of arrogance that would make one think she was some kind of queen.

Corinne Kingman looked her over as though she were a bug that should be stepped on. She strolled closer, not even asking if Ingrid would like to sit down. "I will say one thing," she told Ingrid, studying her more closely. "Jude was right to say you are quite pretty with no color on your face whatsoever, although you certainly could use some."

Ingrid did not know if that was a compliment or an insult.

"Did Jude buy you that dress?" she asked.

"Yes, ma'am. I rushed up here with my dying brother and only the clothes on my back."

The woman snickered. "I'm sure you'll have a closet full of the best dresses you've ever worn once you marry my son—*if* you marry my son."

Ingrid frowned. "If you are saying I would marry him for his money, you are very wrong, Mrs. Kingman. His money and the way he lives are the very reasons I denied my feelings for him for so long. He has apparently told you about his proposal, and that I accepted."

Corinne Kingman looked her over derisively. "Well, I am amazed that you don't see what a ridiculous pair the two of you would make. Our family traces back to English royalty, Miss Svensson, let alone the fact that we are wealthy beyond any measure you could imagine. You would not know how to begin to fit into our lifestyle, and the fact that you surely realize that is why I am here. This visit is for your own good, Miss Svensson."

Ingrid felt her pride creeping up and wanting to make her angry and say things she should not. It was difficult to remember that the woman before her was a child of God. "Are you worried that this lowly Swedish immigrant will embarrass you, Mrs. Kingman?"

The woman smiled. "That is not my reason for coming, Ingrid. May I call you Ingrid?"

"If I may call you Corinne."

A flash of anger spit through the woman's dark brown eyes. "Then I will call you Miss Svensson." She turned and walked back to the window. "It is not the obvious reasons for not marrying my son that I came here to talk about," she told Ingrid. "I came here to ask you something."

"And what is that?"

Corinne turned to face her again. "Think about it. Since there *are* such differences between the two of you, why do you think my son asked you to marry him?"

Ingrid folded her arms. "Because he loves me."

Corinne actually broke into laughter. Ingrid thought her face might break, but it did not. "My dear young lady," the woman told her, "don't be a fool. I know my son. He is handsome, wealthy and well schooled, a man who is sought after by many highborn women. He is a notorious womanizer who has taken advantage of every young lady who has ever thrown herself at him. You are just another conquest."

Ingrid purposely refused to show shock. How could she know if this woman was telling the truth, or if she was lying to discourage her?

"Is that the kind of man you want for a husband?" Mrs. Kingman went on. "Considering the womanizer that he is, why do you think he suddenly wants to marry someone who is far from his type, someone he knows would never be accepted by his family and friends?"

"I told you. For the first time in his life he is in love, Mrs. Kingman. I have shown him a kind of love he has never known."

"You are a fool!" The woman's eyes narrowed. "There is a much simpler answer, Miss Svensson. I am guessing that you have been stringing him along, making him uncertain of your feelings for him."

Ingrid's mouth fell open. "I would never—"

"Don't deny it! You have been reeling him in like a fish on a hook, because you want *everything*—the title and the money!"

Ingrid stiffened. "I want none of those things!" she retorted. "I would never play games with a man, and I would only take a man for a husband because I loved him for who he was, not because of his wealth or importance! Perhaps the same cannot be said for *you!*"

Corinne's eyes widened with indignation. "I should *slap* you for that!" she seethed.

Ingrid struggled not to run from the woman's venom. "Perhaps you should. That was a very un-Christian thing to say, and I apologize. But I do not think you know your son very well, Mrs. Kingman. A woman is not some kind of trophy he wants to win. He is a good man, with a big heart and a longing to be loved—truly loved. And I do love him and plan to devote my life to giving him the love he so sorely longs for."

An odd look of victory came into Mrs. Kingman's eyes then. "Jude really has you figured out, doesn't he?" She shook her head. "Miss Svensson, Jude has only ever had to snap his fingers and women would fall at his feet. He told me that you have been very reluctant to take up with him, and I suspect that has frustrated him—so much so that he would go to any lengths to make you his, including marrying you. Once the challenge is gone and he realizes what a foolish thing he's done, he will become bored with you and throw you away like so much trash!" She stepped even closer. "And do not think that you will somehow gain financially. Jude has a law degree, not to mention that this family can afford the most expensive lawyers there are. You would end up with nothing—nothing but shame in realizing you have been used and then thrown away! I am sure he has filled your head with all kinds of sweet words and has even pretended that he will change for you. And now he has gone so far as to pay for your brother's surgery and help you out in many other ways. He is very clever in that respect, Miss Svensson. I am warning you not to fall for his fake love and devotion. And even if the marriage lasted any length of time, you can be sure that he'll *never* give up the life he lives, and you, my dear, would be miserable and out of place in *our* world."

The woman walked over and picked up her cape, tossing it around her shoulders, then taking up her muff and moving her hands into it.

"You give it some thought, Miss Svensson. You will realize that I am right."

With that the woman marched out of the room, leaving Ingrid standing there speechless. Ingrid walked to the window, where she could see Mrs. Kingman step outside and climb into a large, very fine carriage driven by a man wearing a black suit and a top hat.

So, she'd finally met the high-and-mighty Mrs. Jefferson Kingman. She wondered if the woman's husband and possibly Jude's brother had sent her, or if she'd made the decision on her own to come here and discourage a marriage between Ingrid and Jude.

How she wished Jude were here right now. She needed to see the look of love in his eyes, to once again be sure it was real.

Was Mrs. Kingman telling the truth about his real reason for marrying her?

"No" she said softly to herself. She could not and would not believe it.

If Jude's brother thought it was all right to kill to get what he wanted, then perhaps their mother was also capable of lying and intimidating to get what *she* wanted. And now that Ingrid had met the woman, she felt so sorry for Jude because of how he must have grown up. Surely he'd not been shown an ounce of real motherly love.

Corinne Kingman reminded her of the serpent in the story of Adam and Eve, making subtle suggestions, whispering temptations, telling lies to get what Satan wanted.

One thing was certain. If Jude truly was the cad

the woman made him out to be, Ingrid could understand what had made him that way.

She closed her eyes. "God help him. Give him the strength and wisdom to do the right thing."

What was happening back in Chicago? Would he really come back to accompany her to Omaha?

She was totally and desperately in love now, and after meeting Jude's mother, she wanted more than ever to hold him, to give him the love he'd never known. No wonder she'd often seen the look of a miserable little boy in Jude's dark eyes.

Chapter Twenty-Nine

Early March

Ingrid gave Johnny another teaspoon of laudanum and tucked him into the luxurious bed in Jude's Pullman car in which they would ride back to Omaha. The trip from the hospital to the waiting train had jostled Johnny enough to cause a headache, but she tried not to worry, as the doctor predicted that would happen.

"Try to sleep, Johnny. We'll be in Omaha in no time."

"Thanks, Ingrid," he answered weakly. "And

thank Mr. Kingman for this bed. Why is he being so nice to us?"

"Because he is a better man than you thought, Johnny, and he wants to help." Ingrid glanced at the elderly nurse who sat on the other side of Johnny. "I will leave him to you now, Mrs. Thomas."

"You don't need to fuss over him so, Miss Svensson," the gray-haired nurse told her with a smile. "I'll take good care of him. Mr. Kingman hired me so you could relax."

Yes, Jude had thought of everything. Ingrid left Johnny's bed and walked into the main parlor, where Jude sat reading a newspaper. He'd come back to accompany her, just as he'd promised. They had embraced joyfully, kissed tenderly, but then there had been so much fussing over Johnny that they'd hardly had time yet to talk about what was weighing on her mind: their love and Jude's mother's visit. At first Ingrid was so glad to see him return that she'd instantly put aside all the terrible things Corinne Kingman had told her, but now it was time to confront them.

"Come sit down and relax," Jude told her, waving her over to a velvet love seat.

Ingrid walked across the rich carpeting of the opulent Pullman, thinking how a queen couldn't travel much better than this. Her own head aching with tension and indecision, she sat down beside Jude and leaned her head back, feeling so very tired. "It will be good to get home to my plain little house, but it will be hard seeing Far's things there."

"I'm sure it will. You just let me know as soon as you think Johnny is well enough to attend a memorial service."

She sighed deeply. "Jude, I cannot keep asking you to leave important business just to help me out with things."

He reached for a glass of water beside him. "That's what people do for each other when they're in love. I could give you the world, Ingrid Svensson, if you wanted it, but I know you don't." He sipped some water and set it aside, leaning forward to rest his elbows on his knees. "Now, why don't you tell me what's wrong?"

Ingrid frowned. "What?"

"In spite of our embrace, I felt the coolness in your reception when I arrived at the hospital this morning, and ever since then you have made a point to occupy all your time tending to Johnny and pretending you didn't have time for me, even though we've brought a nurse along to help. Something is bothering you, Ingrid, and I want to know what it is. Something has changed since I first left you. And please don't tell me you've decided not to marry me. I am getting to the point where I can't imagine my life without you, and I've made up my mind. I love you, and that's all there is to it."

She watched his dark eyes closely. Never had she seen deceit there. Still...

She cast her eyes down. "You truly don't know?"

"Know what?"

She swallowed. "I had a visit from your mother."

There came several long seconds of silence, and when Ingrid met his eyes again, she saw anger there.

"My *mother*?"

"Yes. And I can certainly understand why you have often talked about her in a derisive way. It's too bad. A person should honor and respect his or her parents. Christ teaches that we must. It is even in the Ten Commandments. But I can see where she can be a very cruel woman when she wants to be. I am sorry for you, Jude."

He stood up, fists clenched. "What did she say to you? Did she insult you?"

His ire was building. "Jude, it's all right. I would expect her to try to discourage me from marrying you."

"What did she tell you that has made you so distant?" he insisted.

She looked down and toyed with the tiny pink bows that decorated another of the lovely day dresses he'd bought for her to wear. "I can't really say. It's—it's rather embarrassing."

"Embarrassing?"

She rolled her eyes, still looking away. "It was about—other women. She said there have been many and that I was just another prize for you. She said when you were through with me, you would throw me away like so much trash."

His rage was so great that Ingrid could feel it in the air. When she dared glance at him, his dark eyes darted in her direction and held her gaze with their fury.

"And you *believed* her?"

She wanted to cry. "I don't know *what* to believe. I know nothing about your world, Jude, or your past. You have everything a woman would want in a man, and you are skilled at getting your way, and—"

He let out a pitiful groan, running a hand through his hair.

"Jude, I only know that I love the Jude Kingman I've known less than a year. What about your life before that? And how far will you go to get your way?"

He paced for several seconds, then faced her,

breathing heavily in an apparent attempt to control his anger. "Ingrid, I'm not saying I have a perfect past, but my mother had no right talking like that. And I'm a changed man now. *You* did that for me. You're the one who talks about forgiveness, Ingrid, so I need you to forgive the man I *used* to be, and love the man I am *now*. My mother is furious that I want to marry you, and she'd do anything to stop it. Can't you see that? I won't let it happen. I told you I'd move to Omaha and live a more modest life. I meant that. I've never known the happiness I've known with you. I don't ever want to lose that. And you've said yourself that true love means trust. *Trust*, Ingrid! You've got to *trust* me!"

She saw pure sincerity in his eyes. "I don't need to forgive you for something that happened before we even met, Jude. Just tell me there has been no one else since then, that there is no one in Chicago—"

"*No* one! Since I met you there hasn't been any-one else. I haven't *wanted* anyone else. And never once have I truly been in love as I am now. You must believe me." He walked closer, kneeling in front of her. "You bring me peace, Ingrid, a deep peace inside. I never knew how love felt till now."

She saw a pleading look in his gaze.

"What my mother did was wrong and under-handed." He looked away and stood up, rubbing at his neck. "I should have known she'd pull something like this. She tries to control people's lives." He walked over and sat down beside her again, taking her hand. "I love you, Ingrid. I don't know what more I can do to make you believe that. You've changed my life, and I thank God every day for bringing us together. Believe me, the old Jude Kingman would never say these things to *any* woman."

He took something from his jacket pocket, then held a small box in front of her. "I've deliberately learned the Swedish custom of engagement, Ingrid. That should show you how sincere I am. There are two rings in this box, one for me and one for you. You'll get a second ring when you marry me. And I knew you wouldn't accept an expensive diamond, so these are just two simple gold rings. I'm so sorry my mother had to go and spoil this moment. I have had this planned all week."

Ingrid drew in her breath, taking the box with shaking hands and opening it. There inside, against black velvet, lay two gold rings, one a man's, one a woman's. He did love her! "You went to the trouble of finding out our custom for engagement and marriage?"

"Enough to know that the bride and groom walk

down the aisle together instead of just the bride. Walk down the aisle with me, Ingrid."

He was so sincere, and she could not help believing that a man like Jude surely would not humble himself this way and offer her these rings if his feelings were not real. She closed the box without taking her ring.

"I do not want to be the cause of you feeling you must choose between me or your family."

He put the box in her hand. "You aren't the one forcing me to make that choice. *They* are." He leaned close and kissed her cheek. "My family needs to understand that this is real and that I'll be living a different sort of life. I'll transfer everything to Omaha and that's where we'll live and start our life together. Nothing is going to change that, Ingrid."

Ingrid studied his eyes. How could she not love and marry this man? "It's been so hard to believe that all this is real." She touched his face. "The rings are lovely. I am so touched, Jude."

He took her hand and kissed her palm. "Then say it again, for once and for all. Say you love me, and that you will marry me, no matter what. Put the ring on."

She smiled through tears. "I love you, and I will marry you, no matter what, but—"

"What is it?"

"Once we get Johnny settled and the nurse can care for him, I think we should go back to Chicago together, Jude, and face your family with our love. They should know they can always remain a part of our lives and our children's lives if they so choose. We have to make at least one effort to mend the hard feelings and misunderstandings."

He turned away. "I won't submit you to their insults."

"One time, Jude. We have to face them together at least one time. Then we will know we tried."

He put his face in his hands. "I don't want you seeing Mark again. It would bring back the tragedy of Carl and how he died."

"God alone will deal with Mark. I am not afraid to face him or your mother or Jefferson Kingman. I want them to see how much we love each other and know that they cannot come between us. What your mother did was wrong, and we must tell her so. I want to see your world, Jude, your home, your—"

He waved her off. "No, you don't. Believe me, you don't."

Ingrid rose, walking over to take his hands. "Jude, you know just about everything there is to know about me and my world. But I still feel removed from yours. If we are to marry, you have to let me into that world and let me make myself known there, too."

He pulled her into his arms, sighing deeply. "I'm afraid that if you see the family mansion and the way I've lived all my life, you'll decide this isn't right after all. I'm afraid I'll lose you if I take you there."

She met his eyes. "You spoke a moment ago of trust. Now *you* need to trust *me*—to trust that I love the person you are and not your outer world. I promise you it will make no difference to me, and I will feel better knowing we faced your family together. It will show them you are not ashamed of marrying me, and that I am not afraid of them or their power or that world you come from. If this is real, Jude, then God is in control. He will guide us through this, and we must both trust Him to bring a resolution to all this conflict. We need to let your mother know there is no use trying to stop this, because it is God's will. It is no longer even in our power to stop it. We love each other too much."

He studied her fondly. "Then put on the ring, and I will wear mine. If we are going to see them, then I want to be wearing the promise rings."

She opened the box again and took out her ring. "Put it on me, Jude, and I will never remove it."

His eyes teared as he took the ring and slipped

it on her finger. She then took his ring and put it on his. She looked up at him. "There. Now nothing can come between us."

He slowly nodded. "Nothing." He sealed the promise with a kiss.

The Lord guides a man in the way he should go
And protects those who please him.
If they fall, they will not stay down,
Because the Lord will help them up.

Psalms 37:23-24

Chapter Thirty

Ingrid grasped Jude's hand as he helped her disembark the taxi carriage that had brought them from the train station to north Chicago.

"Wait for us," Jude told the carriage driver. "We won't be staying long."

The driver nodded, and Ingrid pulled her cape closer around her against the cool March weather. She'd chosen to wear her own clothes rather than something fancier Jude would have bought for her. She wanted nothing pretentious about her appearance when facing Jude's parents. She was who she was, and they needed to accept that.

Now she wondered how easy it would be to face them after all. "Oh, my!" was all she could say as she studied the huge, ornate Kingman mansion, much more a castle than a warm and welcoming home. The brick structure sat on the banks of Lake Michigan, and it loomed threateningly before them as Jude led Ingrid along the brick walkway that led to the huge double front doors. The grounds were perfectly groomed, and this very moment several Chinese people were at work cleaning up twigs and branches that had fallen over the winter.

Before Jude reached for the doorknob, Jefferson Kingman himself opened one of the doors, motioning Jude and Ingrid to come quickly inside.

"Where's the butler?" Jude asked.

Jefferson scowled as he closed the door. "Your mother doesn't want anyone to know about this, if possible, not even the servants."

Jude moved an arm around Ingrid. "Know about what?" He raised his voice then, so that it echoed throughout the huge marble entranceway and up a winding staircase. "That I am marrying Ingrid Svensson?" he yelled.

Jefferson stiffened. "How dare you! Come into my office."

"This is my home, Ingrid," Jude told her, keeping his voice loud as they followed Jefferson. "If you can call it a home. It's more like a giant ware-house where expensive paintings and furnishings are kept. I have one whole wing to myself, kind of like a house within a house. This place is a bit larger than your little log cabin, wouldn't you say? Oh, but not nearly as warm and inviting." He leaned down and kissed her cheek. "You all right?" he asked softly. "We can leave right now if you want."

"I am a bit overwhelmed by...all this." She looked around the three-story entranceway, stud-ied the grand chandelier hanging high above. "But I'm fine." She clung to his arm as Jude led her over a marble floor that echoed every skirt rustle and every footstep.

"I'd show you each of the twelve bedrooms and the grand kitchen and the den and the smoking room and the several offices and the library and the parlor and the massive third-floor ballroom and the balconies and my wing and the dining room with a table that serves fifty people at one sitting—" he sighed mockingly "—but then we don't have a week, do we? We only have a few minutes."

He led her through the huge wooden door that led into a high-ceilinged office with bookshelves that were stuffed clear to the ceiling. A rolling lad-der was attached to the top shelf so one could climb up to retrieve whatever book one chose. Jefferson Kingman was already seated behind a grand, beautifully carved oak desk, so large that he looked almost ridiculously small behind it, especially since the leather chair was far too big for a man his size.

There came a rustling sound behind them to the right after they entered the room, and Jude and Ingrid both turned to see Corinne Kingman standing there, her dark eyes glowering. She gave the grand oak door a shove so that it slammed shut with intimidating force, then strutted closer to Jude and Ingrid.

She regarded her son. "So, you dare to bring this foreign, uneducated farm woman into this house, after I begged you not to do such a thing!"

Jude grinned. "I told you in my telegram that we were coming and why. You can scream at us and hate us all you like, but although you certainly don't act it, Corinne, you are my mother—" he turned to Jefferson "—and you are my father, and Ingrid, being the good, Christian woman that she is, wants you to know that no matter how you treat her, she respects you as my parents and you will always be welcome in our home in Omaha." He turned and bowed slightly to his mother. "Humble as it might be."

"Humble!" Corinne sniffed. "You—a King-

man—living like a commoner! How are we supposed to explain that?" She glared at Ingrid. "I
thought I got it through your simple head that this
can't last and that you are nothing but a novel interest to Jude, one he'll tire of quickly and cast
aside like—"

"Don't you say another word, Corinne!" Jude
said then, his light banter gone. The sharp com-
mand made Corinne stiffen and back away.

"Tell Ingrid you're sorry," Jude ordered.

"What?"

"Tell her you're sorry for the lies you told her
about me, and for going to see Ingrid against my
wishes and trying to destroy the most beautiful
love I've ever known."

Corinne Kingman pressed her lips together,
turning away. "I am *not* sorry for trying to keep my
son from becoming a laughingstock." She faced
Jude again. "If you really care about this girl,
you'll—"

"I *do* care! That's why we're here."

"Jude and I are very much in love, Mrs. Kingman," Ingrid spoke up. "I wanted to come here and
see where Jude is from, talk with both of you together and assure you—"

"You're not getting a dime of Kingman
money!" Corinne interrupted. "That is the only

reason we allowed Jude to bring you here, to tell you flat out that you won't get a thing out of this and that we will never acknowledge your existence. If Jude wants to marry the likes of you, then he is out of our lives!"

The woman turned and marched over to a velvet and cherrywood chair, where she took a seat, refusing to look at either of them. Ingrid felt Jude's arm tighten around her. "I *told* you this was a bad idea." He led Ingrid to a chair across from his father's desk. "Please sit."

Ingrid sat down, not quite sure what to expect. Jude turned to his mother. "Insult Ingrid one more time, Mother dear, and I will splash our marriage all over the Chicago papers in bold, black letters. I'll make headlines out of it!"

Corinne gasped.

Jude turned to his father. "Ingrid wanted this, not me. She sincerely wants you to know that even though you may cut us out of your lives, we will not cut you out of ours. If you can't understand and respect that kindness, then there is not one thing or one person in this house I will miss, Father." He looked around. "Where is Mark?"

Jefferson appeared a bit subdued. "He had business in New York."

"How convenient. I was told he was home just

yesterday. He's been avoiding me like the plague for months. I think you and I both know why that is, Father, and why he made it a special point not to be here when he knew I'd be bringing Ingrid for a—what is this anyway—a visit? And what a pleasant one it is. It might have been even more pleasant if Mark were here to face Ingrid, but then his guilt over murdering her friends and neighbors would have made that impossible."

Jefferson Kingman cast a warning look toward his son, but Jude just glared at him.

"Jude, it's all right. We've said what we came to say. Perhaps we should go now." Ingrid started to rise.

"No," Jude answered. "Now maybe you see why I like the idea of a small, simple house, Ingrid—a home where family members don't live in rooms so far apart that they don't even see each other for days at a time. A family should be close, should share the same dinner table. And brothers should be treated equally by their parents." He turned to Corinne again. "Isn't that right, Mother dear? But it's never been like that in this...this excuse of a home has it?"

"What was really your point in coming here, Jude?" Jefferson asked with a severe frown. "Did you honestly expect us to be glad for your happy little life with your simple little wife in your plain little house? Is that it?" He rose. "Go on with you. You know what a busy man I am."

"Well, Dad, it's Sunday. Seems to me you shouldn't be all that busy on a Sunday. Did you and Mother go to church this morning?"

Clearly irritated, Jefferson answered crisply. "Of course we did."

Jude smiled, nodding his head. "Of course. Did you pray, Dad? I mean, *really* pray? Did you ask God what you should do about my marriage, ask God to help you accept Ingrid for the beautiful, wonderful woman she is? Did you ask God to help you deal with what you know about Mark?"

"You have no right bringing that up!" Corinne spouted.

"I think I do! As long as Ingrid and I are here, we might as well clear the air about a lot of things. The minute you insulted Ingrid when we came in this room I knew there was more that needed to be said than just inviting you to our wedding."

Ingrid ached for Jude. His life here had been even more loveless than she'd realized. It was obvious by his parents' attitudes. And now she realized that what his brother did still ate at him.

"Will you just get to the point, Jude?" Jefferson demanded. "And before you start throwing insults and accusations at your brother, I will remind you that he is not here to defend himself, and that he is our son! You don't have children of your own yet. You have no idea what lengths a father and mother will go to to protect their own, no matter what they have done wrong!"

Jude folded his arms, showing not the least bit of intimidation. "When something is the truth, it can no longer be just an insult or an accusation. It's simple fact, one that all of you have to live with. I can already see that Mark is having trouble doing that, since he no longer speaks to me or wants to face me. So I will let the Good Lord decide how that matter is to be settled among the three of you and how you all choose to live with it. I can't prove anything, and I almost lost my life because people thought I was the one responsible. I have a question about my own shooting, and I want the truth. Are you two capable of being honest with me?"

"What on earth are you talking about?" Corinne demanded.

"What I'm talking about, Mother dear, is the distinct feeling that you and father would not have greatly grieved if I'd died from that gunshot wound. Why do you think that is?"

"What gives you that outrageous idea?" Corinne asked.

"Well, let's see. Maybe the fact that you didn't even visit me when I was first brought home. You were too busy with some kind of social event. And maybe it's because you two might as well have only one son, as far as I am concerned, and I'd really like to know why. Let's get it all out in the open, as long as Ingrid is here. She wanted to understand this side of my life, but I suddenly realize that there is some of it I don't even understand myself. Ingrid is the most honest, honorable woman I've ever known, and if she's going to take me for a husband, she needs to know everything there is to know about me and this family."

Ingrid sensed the deep hurt in Jude's soul, and she silently prayed for him. She noticed Corinne look at Jefferson as though deeply worried about something.

Jefferson sighed, taking a cigar from an ornate silver box. He walked to a marble fireplace at the side of the room and lit the cigar with a long match. "I should have had the maid light this fireplace," he commented absently. "It's chilly in here."

"Yes, it certainly is," Jude replied, taking a chair across from the desk, close to Ingrid.

Jefferson turned to face him. "What's *really* brought all of this on, Jude?"

"What's brought this on, Dad, is that I am getting married. I want my future wife to know the real Jude Kingman and to have no doubts as to my love for her. I want to resolve these personal issues so Ingrid can be sure that I love her for her, not because I'm just longing for something that's been missing from my life. I have always felt like an outsider in this family and was always the one who could never please you, in spite of the fact that I've never done one thing to disgrace you or disappoint you. I would really like to know why."

"Jude, surely you see what a foolish decision you've made," Jefferson told him.

Corinne rose and walked over to face her husband. "This is *your* fault! You brought him into this family and from day one he hasn't behaved like a true Kingman! Now he will embarrass us beyond repair! How are we to explain this?"

Amazed, Ingrid stared at the woman Jude had called mother all his life. What a strange remark to make: *you brought him into this family.* What did that mean? She turned to Jude, who looked as though someone had slugged him in the chest. He, too, realized the possible meaning of his mother's remark. Was he not a true son by blood?

"Be quiet, Corinne," Jefferson told his wife. "Maybe you should go lie down and let me handle this."

"Handle what?" Jude asked, now rising from his chair. "What did she mean about you bringing me into this family, about me never behaving like a true Kingman?"

"Let it go, Jude."

"No, Dad. This is a bit of a revelation, wouldn't you say? When I marry Ingrid, I want to feel totally free of emotional burdens that might keep us from being truly happy. Even Ingrid can see there is something deeply wrong here. What is going on?"

"Jude—"

"The *truth*, Dad! A man's firstborn son shouldn't be treated the way I'm treated!"

"You're *not* our firstborn son!" The words came from Corinne.

"Shut up!" Jefferson told her.

Ingrid was astonished, both at Jefferson for talking to his wife that way, and at Corinne's stunning statement. She rose and stood beside Jude, who was beginning to pale.

"What are you talking about?" Jude asked his mother. "Mark was born first? Am I younger than Mark? Why would you lie about something like that? Was I an unwanted baby?"

"*Yes!*" Corinne spat at him. She turned then and fled the room, crying.

Ingrid gasped with agony for Jude, who stood

there looking confused. He turned to his father, and Ingrid felt at least a grain of relief at seeing genuine sorrow in Jefferson's eyes.

"Well, Dad, for the first time in my whole life I can see a spark of feeling in your eyes," Jude told him. "This must be a really heavy bit of news to create a hint of emotion in your stoic personality. What is it you don't want to tell me?"

Jefferson walked over to lay his cigar in an ashtray. He rubbed his eyes as though very weary.

"Sit down, Jude," he said gruffly, as he himself walked over to sit behind his desk again. "You, too, Miss Svensson. Since you intend to marry Jude, you need to hear this, too. You might even change your mind about a wedding."

Ingrid reached over and grasped Jude's hand. "I will never change my mind, Mr. Kingman. My love for Jude has nothing to do with this family or his past or anything you have to tell me about him."

"Is that so?" Jefferson leaned back. "Well then, you won't be upset to learn that Jude is not a Kingman at all. I, uh, I...bought him."

The room grew dead silent, and Jude pulled his hand away, rising from his chair. "*Bought* me?"

Ingrid saw his hands move into fists.

"Promise me this will stay among you and me and Ingrid, Jude," Jefferson told him. "You and this woman want the truth, and with all that's happened I suppose you deserve to hear it."

"I'm not making any promises of secrecy!"

"You *must* promise!" Jefferson stood up again and began pacing. "I'm laying Corinne's and my reputation and good standing on the line here!" He walked to the fireplace again, rubbing at the back of his neck. "If it weren't for your foolish desire to marry this...this farm woman, none of this would have come up!"

"Don't blame this on Ingrid! I've been tormented for years over the odd way you two treat me. Meeting Ingrid only brought to light just how starved I am for love and how I long for a normal family life. So go ahead, Dad—or should I call you that? Tell me the truth. I'll even promise it will go no further than this room. Ingrid can be trusted, which is more than I can say for you and Corinne!" He let out an odd, groaning gasp. "I knew money could buy a lot of things, but this—"

He walked over to the door as though he wished to run away. Ingrid longed to go to him, ached for his suffering, sure he must be feeling as gray and cold and hopeless as the dreary March weather.

Jefferson let out a long sigh and cleared his throat before speaking. He glanced at Ingrid, looking somewhat embarrassed now, then turned his gaze to Jude. "When our first baby was born, Jude, he was badly deformed, so deformed that Corinne couldn't bear to look at him. She was mortified—thought she'd disappointed me, let me down. She was petrified that the general public would find out, and she begged me to find a way to get rid of the baby and replace it with a healthy one that she could brag to others about."

What an ugly picture the man was presenting. *God help Jude understand this,* Ingrid prayed. *Help both of us deal with this in a Christian way.*

"And I was that healthy baby," Jude said, more as a statement than a question.

Looking completely and surprisingly ashamed, Jefferson nodded. "I—bought you from a destitute young woman who needed the money and didn't want you."

"Where is she now?"

"I have no idea. She's probably dead from poverty and disease, or maybe even from abuse. She was a—" Jefferson glanced at Ingrid again. "Excuse the word, Miss Svensson, but Jude's mother was a prostitute."

Jude emitted another groan. Ingrid rose and walked over to where he stood. "Jude, it's all right."

She saw him fighting tears as he walked away from her and faced his father.

"Obviously, then, no one knows who my father was, which makes me illegitimate. What a pleasant bit of news for Ingrid to hear."

"You came here asking questions and I am answering them. If that farm woman still wants to marry you after this, then maybe she really *does* love you for the right reasons. Isn't that what you wanted to know?"

Jude snickered, walking to a window and refusing to look at Ingrid. "Well, well," he said, "everything is finally beginning to make sense." He faced his father again. "What happened to the poor, helpless, deformed baby? What happened to your *real* son, Jefferson?"

Jefferson closed his eyes. "He was put in an institution, where he died a few months later."

"Probably of neglect. Those institutions are notoriously inhumane."

"Jude, his life would have been meaningless. Not only were his limbs deformed but he had a cleft palate, and he was blind. Heaven only knows what was wrong on the inside. He simply would not have made it even with the best of care."

Jude finally looked at Ingrid. "There. You see the kind of people my supposed parents are?" He faced his father again, obviously enraged. "You could have *afforded* the best of care! But instead you put your own offspring into an institution where he was left to die!" He shook his head and waved Jefferson away. "I'm almost glad to learn your blood doesn't run in my veins! I'm *very* glad to know Mark Kingman isn't my blood brother at all! What a relief *that* is," he said mockingly. "And how, may I ask, did you manage to keep all of this a secret all these years?"

"When you have money, you can buy silence."

Jude laughed derisively. "Of course. That was a stupid question."

"Jude, if there is any of this you don't believe, you can ask Doc Bellinger. He delivered the baby."

Jude shook his head. "Oh, I believe you. This explains all the unanswered questions. It explains why I could never please either of you, why I never felt loved. I was just a, uh, a proxy, I guess you'd call me. And by the way, what about *my* name? Since I'm not really a Kingman, what should I be calling myself?"

Jefferson studied him sadly. "You are legally a Kingman, and legally you have claim to whatever inheritance any son would get. I don't know what your last name would have been if I had not adopted you, and I don't intend to change your name because of this. I just want you to understand our feelings for Mark, Jude. Can you for one min-

ute put yourself in our shoes? When Mark was
born, we were both terrified at how it might turn
out. When he was born perfectly healthy we were
overjoyed. We had a son of our own, a true heir.
The whole thing with the first child so traumatized
Corinne that I feared she would take her own life.
When she became with child again, she wanted to
get rid of it, she was so afraid. I talked her into carrying the baby, and we felt such joy and pride
when he was born. He healed a huge hole in your
mother's heart."

"Don't call her my mother!" Jude said angrily,
stepping closer. "She obviously never wanted to *be*
my mother and has never had an ounce of feeling
for me. No wonder it was always the nanny who
read to me and cared for me, while Mark was
smothered with love when we were little." He pretended to laugh, but Ingrid could see him fighting
tears. He rubbed at his lips and sniffed, taking a
deep breath before continuing. Ingrid wanted to
weep at the sight of a tear that made its way down
Jude's cheek. "I don't want my supposed legal inheritance, Jefferson," he told the elder Kingman.
"I want absolutely nothing more from this family,
nor do I want any part of any of the businesses.
And even if Ingrid decides not to marry me after
finding out about my lurid beginnings, I am still

leaving Chicago—anyplace away from here and away from you and especially away from Mark. You can tell your friends and fellow businessmen anything you want about why I left. It makes no difference to me. I'll keep your sick little secret, and, uh—" He glanced at Ingrid, biting his lip against his emotions. "And I'll even go along with Ingrid's original reason for coming here. If you ever decide you still want to be a part of our lives, I'll do my best at fighting the hatred I feel right now and will try to forgive and forget, only because that's what Ingrid would want."

Jefferson closed his eyes. "I hope you will try to understand Corinne, Jude. You think I know nothing about love, but I do love Corinne. You have to realize that she was raised by a woman even stricter than Corinne about what's right and proper in the social world. You never knew your grandmother."

"She's not my grandmother anyway, and I have a feeling it's a good thing I *didn't* know her."

A subdued Jefferson Kingman rubbed at his eyes again. "Henrietta Charleston raised Corinne by English standards and drilled it into her head that appearances and perfection mean everything. When that baby was born, Corinne didn't want her mother to know it was deformed. She begged me to find a baby to replace it as quickly as possible."

Jude closed his eyes and shook his head. "You know, it's sinful to raise a child the way I was raised. I'll never do that to a child of mine, even if I end up having to adopt."

Ingrid's heart went out to him. She loved him more than ever, and she could already see Jude Kingman would be a wonderful father who would try to make up for all the love he'd never known growing up.

Surprisingly, Jefferson's own eyes teared. "I'm truly sorry, Jude. I never meant for you to find out any of this."

"You did me a disservice by *not* telling me. I'm glad to know the truth, except that it could cost me the only woman I've ever loved."

"It won't, Jude," Ingrid spoke up. She rushed to his side. "I don't care where you really came from, and I certainly do not care that you are not a King-man. That was never a part of what I love about you, so it does not matter." She faced him, grasping his arms. "Don't you see? You are free, Jude, free of all the wondering, free of having to live up to what you think this family wants of you, free of feeling guilty for sharing the same blood as your brother. You are free to love and be loved. God has opened the door to a whole new life for you, one of love and forgiveness and grace to be who you are, to love whom you choose. I have never loved you more, Jude. Don't let this news destroy what we have found together."

Jude quickly wiped at another tear, looking embarrassed over his emotions. He turned away. "Leave us alone for a few minutes, will you, Jefferson?" he asked.

Jefferson nodded, and Ingrid could see he was truly sorry. He walked past her and close to Jude. "I'm telling you the truth, Jude, when I say that I am glad you found someone like Miss Svensson here. I can see she truly is worthy, that she truly loves you. After what I've told you, I'm glad you have someone like her to lean on. And deep inside I've been rather envious of your good-heartedness—envious because I wished Mark could have been more like you."

He touched Jude's shoulder, then headed for the door.

"Wait!" Jude called out.

Jefferson turned.

"Does Mark know about all of this?"

"No. Let's keep it that way."

Jude sighed deeply. "Your secret is safe with me."

Jefferson nodded. "Thank you." He turned and left, closing the door behind him.

Jude turned to Ingrid. "Unbelievable, yet so believable," he told her. "So many things make so much sense now." A look of deep sadness came into his dark eyes. "I am so sorry—and so embarrassed."

"Sorry for what, Jude? You've not done one thing wrong, and you have absolutely nothing about which to be embarrassed. You are a victim of selfish greed and sinful lies. None of us has any choice over how we are brought into this world, or how those responsible for our welfare raise us."

"Ingrid, our children will be fathered by a bastard. We won't even be able to tell them truthful stories about their paternal grandparents."

"When our children are old enough to know the truth, we will tell them, gently and lovingly. They will think no less of their father because they will love you with all their hearts, Jude, and with no strings attached, because you will be the best father a child can have. Together we will teach them about God's grace and forgiveness, and that all of us are equal in God's eyes, no matter what our past or our beginnings. This changes nothing, Jude, at least not for me. I still want to marry you, and I have every confidence that you will be a good influence for Johnny and help him grow into a fine young man."

He stepped closer, taking her hand and looking down at the promise ring he'd put on her finger. "I had no idea why God brought you into my life, Ingrid, until now. He knew I had to learn the truth, and He knew that once I did learn, I'd need someone like you to help me through it." He pulled her close. "It's just that you're so pure and innocent and you deserve better than me."

She rested her head against his chest. "With you I have *more* than I deserve. Let's go home, Jude, to Omaha, to Johnny. Let's go get married— as soon as possible."

"As soon as possible? Really?"

She nodded her head against his chest.

He pressed her close, and she felt her heart break into pieces when he shook in sobs.

"God, it hurts," he whispered.

"I know," she said softly. "But now you are free, Jude. We both are free to love each other, to create our own world together. You are the one who once told me to follow my heart, and my heart keeps leading me back to you, in spite of the way we met, in spite of our different worlds, in spite of what we know now about who you really are. Indeed, the fact that we can overcome those obstacles makes our being together that much more meaningful. My heart leaves me no choice but to marry you. I can no longer imagine my life without you in it."

They stood there quietly, just holding each other, until Jude was able to find his voice again. He finally pulled away, wiping at tears with his fingers and walking back to the window.

"I'm, uh, I'm thinking of a hymn I've heard. They sang it once in a while at the church I attended growing up, and it meant nothing to me because no one taught me its true meaning. I also heard the congregation at that little church in Plum Creek singing it." He took a deep breath, taking a handkerchief from his pocket and blowing his nose before continuing. "For some reason the words stuck in my head, and for the first time in my life I understand them."

Ingrid struggled against her own tears. "What was the hymn?"

He continued watching out the window. "'Amazing Grace,' I believe it's called."

Ingrid smiled. "'How sweet the sound, that saved a wretch like me.'"

He turned to her, looking like a little boy. "'I once was lost, but now am found,'" he continued. "'Was blind, but now I see.' I do see, Ingrid. I see all that is truly important in life, and she is standing before me, by the grace of God."

Ingrid walked closer, taking his hand. "Let's go home. Johnny needs us, and we have to get him well as quickly as possible so we can be married."

Jude smiled through tears, and together they walked out, across the hard, cold marble floor, through the front door and to the waiting cab.

Chapter Thirty-One

April 2, 1874

It was a simple wedding, in a small church in Omaha. Wilson Beyers attended, as did Matt Oberhue and his family, and Lilly Winters and her husband. A few other customers Ingrid once waited on at Oberhue's were there, and a few railroad workers who'd known Ingrid's father. Johnny waited at the front of the church, and as was Swedish custom, Jude himself walked Ingrid down the aisle.

Ingrid doubted any woman could boast a more handsome groom, and she'd never felt more beautiful than in the cream-colored gown she wore, tailored just for her. Jude had insisted on being allowed to hire someone to make the gown for her, and on ordering extravagant flowers.

Ingrid clung to Jude's arm as they approached the waiting minister. She did not fear her wedding night, or tomorrow, or what the rest of her life might be like. With Jude it could be nothing but wonderful. Just two weeks ago he'd been baptized in this very church. He glowed with happiness at giving his life to Christ, and Ingrid felt blessed that soon she'd be able to call herself Mrs. Jude Kingman.

They spoke their vows, *for richer, for poorer, in sickness and in health...* She watched Jude's dark eyes and knew he would keep his promises to her, as she would most certainly keep hers to him.

"I now pronounce you Mr. and Mrs. Jude Kingman," the minister said.

Jude leaned close and met her lips in a kiss that promised much more to come. After a modest reception at the church, Johnny would stay with the Oberhues and she and Jude would go home to spend their wedding night alone in their lovely Victorian house, with its three bedrooms, parlor, sewing room, library, dining room and nice-size kitchen where sat Ingrid's proudest possession: a new Concord range of the latest design.

They joyously embraced, and just then, only a block from the church, a Union Pacific chugged past, its wailing whistle crying out as it headed west across Nebraska. Ingrid thought how less than one year ago Far was out checking the fields to see how soon they could plant their rows of corn, while a man named Jude Kingman was on his way to Plum Creek, unaware that his journey would bring him into her life—into her heart—and into God's warm embrace.

* * * * *